Exposed

Book 4 of A New Life Series

Samantha Jacobey

Exposed

Book 4 of A New Life Series

Samantha Jacobey

Lavish Publishing, LLC ~ Houston

First Edition
2015 Lavish Publishing, LLC
Book 4 of A New Life Series
All Rights Reserved
Published in the United States by Lavish Publishing, LLC, Houston
Cover Design by: Nicolene Lorette Design
Cover Images: SHUTTERSTOCK
Paperback ISBN
ISBN: **0692233067**
ISBN-13: **978-0692233061**
www.LavishPublishing.com

Table of Contents

Prologue

"Whaddaya think? Is he tellin' th' truth?" Buck leaned against the support pole, waiting to see what would be their next move.

Brett ran his fingers over his lips, studying the man hanging from the roof in front of them. "Unlikely."

"Want I should beat some sense int' 'im?" he grinned, reaching for his shiny buckle.

"You fat bastard! You really thinks my story's gonna change? Cut me down, le's settle this like men... see how many more teeth you can come up missin'," their victim growled angrily, blood dripping from his chin.

Buck stared back, waiting for his leader to give the word.

"Light him up," Brett muttered and turned to walk away, pulling a cigarette from his pocket with one hand and digging for his Zippo with the other. He could hear the sound of the leather as it ripped into Enrique's flesh. *Damn things are gonna kill me*, he coughed, flipping the lighter closed with a flick of his wrist.

Crushing out the butt beneath the heel of his boot a few minutes later, he made his way back over to their prisoner.

Surveying the fresh wounds that oozed blood down his back, he released a low whistle. "Buck, my friend, I think you enjoy that belt o' yurs too much."

Shifting so that he could make eye contact, "You come up with anything yet? You know I should kill you. All you gotta do is tell me where to find 'er, an' you get to live. Now, don't that sound like a heck of a good deal?"

"I told you," Enrique's chest heaved as he struggled to breathe, "I dunno where she's at... Calls me stupid fur tryin' t' play... you boys like I did... I ain't seen her... since the Dragons was here... swear to God."

"Ya know, I never thought you's a smart man. But even yur not dumbfuck enough to call me up an' tell me you're bringin' me Eddie's prize whore, when ya got no fuckin' clue where she's at!" Brett's voice had been slowly escalating in volume, ending in a full shout, "Tell me where the fuck she is, God dammit!" For emphasis, he kicked his former group mate in the ribs with his knee to punctuate his curses.

Enrique fell into a spasm of coughs, a wad of phlegm and blood spewing out onto the ground in front of him. "Kill me then..." he heaved, "I gots nothin' else to say."

Brett punched him in the ear, scowling in his rage. Turning to storm away, he ran his hand through his curly red hair. Motioning to Buck, "Le's talk."

The pair made their way down the road a couple of hundred yards, well out of earshot of any of the others. "We ain't gettin' nothin' from him. Even if he knows, he ain't gonna tell us." Brett inhaled deeply, blowing the air out through pursed lips. "We need another plan."

"We gonna kill 'im?" Buck tossed his thumb over his shoulder, towards the metal awning, "Or jus' let 'im 'ang till someone finds 'im?"

"Naw, we cut him down. I have another way to find

8

her… jus' may not work's all. Depends on what she knows. Worth a shot though, our only shot really."

Half an hour later, Enrique sat on the stone bench, his gear strewn on the table behind him. His ears were ringing something fierce, and his body ached from the worst beating he had ever taken, but he refused to let them think they'd won. "I guess you believes me now?" he demanded in a surly tone.

"Naw, I think you're a liar. But tha's ok. We're gonna find 'er. An' when we do, I'm gonna give 'er the same beatin' I jus' gave you, jus' t' be fair."

Enrique's head shot up to see Buck sneering down at him. "See? I knew you's lyin'. I sees it in yur eyes, boy. So I make a deal wit ya… you find 'er, an' you bring 'er in, an' I won't make 'er bleed when I lay int' 'er." Buck grinned at him, his tongue pushed through the gaps of his missing teeth in an excited fashion.

Enrique breathed deeply, his mind spinning. Dropping his gaze to stare at the boots of the man in front of him, his heart pounded inside his chest. Taking in ragged breaths, he kept his head down, not daring to look up as the footwear turned and walked away from him. He cringed as he heard the sound of the bikes start up around him and head off down the road, leaving him in a cloud of dust, alone in the late afternoon sun.

What Awaits

Tori sat between the two men in silence. On her right sat her husband, the man of her dreams. *Hell, it could be anyone's dreams really; he's tall, dark and handsome, right?* However, he's also supportive, intelligent and protective - everything a girl could want in a man.

On her left sat her former lover. He's short, conniving, and deceitful. *A man who has lied to me, used me and sent me on my way. So why am I feeling so conflicted?* It had been a year since she had even seen Eli, and so much had happened since then.

Stealing a glance at the man to her left, she noticed his intense glare, boring into the seat in front of him. His brows were furrowed, jaw clenched, obviously deep in angry thought. Allowing her mind to drag the memories of him to the surface, she recalled the first time she had ever seen him, pressing her down into the mattress of a hospital bed to restrain her. *I can still smell the gel in his hair as he held me there.*

She had just regained consciousness after murdering eleven men in a farmhouse in Iowa. That, and she had tried to kill herself. That's what all the liquor had been for; so that she would go to sleep and never have to face another day, filled with the guilt that still haunts her. *Thank God it hadn't worked.*

In the days that followed, Eli had come to visit her. He wanted her to talk, but she wasn't ready for that yet. Wasn't ready to feel and be and live. The hurt was too raw, too new, and all she could do was listen; so he talked.

He shared so much about himself, gave her so much attention. And it wasn't big things either. The little things he did mattered the most; those little cherished moments that stole her heart.

His little book of fairy tales, his little pink rose. He wanted something from her, but he got more than he expected. *He's right. You wanted to be in his bed that night, to make love to him,* she remembered their passion fondly. But she had never been cared for before, never given dignity, so she didn't know any better. He did. *He knew it was wrong. He should have put a stop to it.*

Giving her head a shake to clear it, she swung her gaze away from him. Holding Michael's hand, his fingers entwined with her right and covered by her left, she stroked him with her thumb affectionately.

Staring down at the shiny white gold on her special finger, she recalled how he had walked into her life and how hard she had worked to push him out of it. *God, I hated his being there.* At least at first she did.

Tori mentally retraced the steps of their relationship as if she held her journal and pencil; a much longer trip, the two of them having shared a much deeper, and more tumultuous history.

The couple had met some years ago under ominous circumstances while Tori was still the property of Eddie Farrell. Her life had been chaotic at best, leaving her more of a broken being, only half alive, not capable of thinking beyond the group and its wayward life.

She recalled the day he had hooked up with the crew in a bar in Arkansas. He tried to introduce himself, and she had snubbed him, not liking the fact that he looked so much like Henry, and she wasn't even permitted to ask why. The man had ridden with them for three days and to his credit, he had kept his distance, which only added to her curiosity over him.

Strictly speaking, she knew very little about him at the time; only that he rode with the group for a few days and then disappeared. His presence had intrigued her, leaving her with many questions, but there were few answers to be had. *That, and I assumed that he had fucked me when Eddie awarded me to him as a prize.*

Slowly shaking her head, she recalled that her curiosity over him had brought Eddie's wrath down upon her, and it was basically because of Michael Anderson that she wore a scar across her left eye. *Eddie was sure pissed when I asked what became of him,* and oddly enough, she had thought about the stranger several times over the years in passing. *I never have figured out why.*

On the flip side, there had been things she didn't realize when he joined the group; he had seen her as nothing more than a dirty whore. He had certainly never been with her, even though he had the chance. Recalling what she had since learned about that first encounter, she squeezed his fingers firmly. *He's a real man,* she respected him deeply. *He's a man of honor, trust and loyalty.*

Michael met with the group because Henry, his older brother, had summoned him. He had agreed to help his sibling get her out of the turmoil, striking a secret deal with him. *Henry had loved and cared for me since I was a child, and it was solely out of devotion to him that Michael agreed to look after me.* She might have felt bitter about that fact,

12

but she understood his black and white view of her and her past life.

Jumping forward some four and a half years, Tori recalled how she found herself working in a music shop and living in a halfway house under orders by the FBI. *God, what a nightmare… how does shit like that actually happen?* But in the end, she needed that time to rejoin the human race.

Trying desperately to put her life in order, Tori had learned to accept the help of Terral Huffman, former Fed and owner of Music Maniac, her mentor and friend. This stranger soon became the father she had never known. She had been making headway, and things seemed to be looking up for her. *Terry was a real friend,* she recalled the shop owner tenderly. *I had more in LA than I was ready to admit.*

Thinking she finally had control and ready to plan her own destiny, she received a jolt from the past. Michael, who then worked as the head of personal security for a band putting on a promo at the store, showed up and sent her reeling.

He kept himself at bay a few days, watching her until the right time to confront her. His sudden reappearance spun her into panic mode, and she fled the shop and her life trying to avoid him.

I felt so much fear, like I had never felt before, as I left the store that day. I half expected to be jumped and grabbed… or shot… or stabbed… as soon as I got outside. And I was so afraid something would happen to Terry and the rest of my friends, no matter what I did. She breathed deeply, the memory almost too real at the moment to bear.

But Michael had been alone, and under the weight of his oath to his brother, he refused to let her get away, and caught up to her on a bus headed to Denver. Tori's heart began to pound as she recalled peering up into those chocolate brown eyes as the bus pulled out onto the road. *He looked so much like Henry then, it was like looking into the soul of a ghost.*

It had been so hard, too, keeping him away, pretending like I didn't want him there. The couple had made their way down into the heart of Texas, where they purchased an old gas station and converted it into a shop for rebuilding motorcycles. *Stubborn bastard,* she sneered to herself, *I did every annoying thing I could think of, and he still followed my ass!*

During their travels, Michael had come to see through the stoic façade that the girl used to protect herself, and came to genuinely care for her very deeply. She shifted to peek at him, aware that he watched her, but not ready to break her train of thought.

Together, they had built a life, and in the end, she had to admit she had fallen in love with him as well. They were married on the first of April, a short ten weeks ago. *The craziest, happiest day of my entire existence,* she realized as she fingered her ring fondly. The memory brought a wide smile to her lips as she gripped his hand more firmly. *He loves me for who I truly am, maybe the only person besides Henry, who ever has.*

With a sigh, she considered how their lives would have been perfect except for one thing: *my past.* It wasn't that Michael didn't understand her past or couldn't get over it; he had made his peace with who she was. It wasn't that Tori couldn't let go either, as she had learned to forgive her own transgressions and find where she belonged. The problem was, her past refused to let go of her, looming around them like a dark storm waiting to unleash its fury.

Panting slightly, Tori began to feel more relaxed. She wasn't writing in her journal at that moment, but having made enough entries, she understood the process. Mentally retracing their steps had been sufficient to let her mind be at ease. Adjusting her digits as they grasped those of her mate, she settled into her seat more calmly to consider their current situation, her lips still curving gently.

Beginning to fear what lurked around them, having stayed in one place too long, the couple had planned to head out on Michael's bike that very morning. She briefly pictured his motorcycle, currently locked in the garage, with their bedrolls strapped to the back of it. *It waits for us to climb on and be on our way.*

Instead, they had been picked up by Federal Agent Eli Founder and were being escorted to New York. The purpose of the trip had yet to be revealed, and the couple sat on the plane with him, moving towards whatever awaits them in the big city. Another glance at Eli, she speculated he wasn't going to tell them anything until it served his purpose. *You could take a lesson or two from this guy,* she kidded herself half- heartedly.

Seeing the *fasten seatbelt* symbol light up, she knew they had reached their destination. Looking over at her husband, he still watched her intently, so she gave him a tiny grin and they shared a kiss. Butterflies danced in her chest, reassuring her she had married the right man, and she chose to linger with her face next to his, relishing in the feel of his warm breath on her skin and the small smile on his lips.

Using their German, she spoke softly, "You were right, you know."

"Oh yeah?" he countered, "About what?"

"About love," she smiled, "This is definitely worth it." She pushed her face forward to kiss him again. "I love you, Michael Anderson. Please don't ever forget that," her left hand moved up to grasp a few sandy brown ringlets.

"I know, and I won't. I love you, too." Caressing her side and back with his right hand, they remained in their private moment, holding one another until the plane came to a halt in front of the gate and they could exit the massive craft.

Rags to Riches

Reaching under her seat, Tori retrieved her bag that carried the items she had packed for their road trip, before it was so rudely interrupted. Tossing it over her shoulder, she could see the two men once again exchange angry smirks as they squeezed down the aisle. The three of them made their way out into the tunnel and on through the gate area in silence.

The JFK airport felt as daunting as the others she had seen. Staying close to Michael, fingers still attached, Tori followed the two men as they weaved their way through the crowd. Not having any baggage to claim, they smoothly made their way directly out to the front, where a black Crown Victoria waited for them.

Tori climbed into the back seat and slid across, Michael taking the seat beside her. The door closed with a loud thud, and Eli shuffled into the front passenger seat, closing his door with an equally heavy slam. She looked over at him sharply, noting his face tense and he clenched his jaw repeatedly. She could tell he still fumed inside, but felt no sympathy for him. *He made his bed and now he's gonna have to lie in it.*

"So, are you gonna tell us where you're taking us?" Michael spoke up, staring at the back of Eli's head and resisting the urge to injure the man in front of him.

Eli kept his eyes fixed on the traffic, making no effort to reply and Tori maintained her claim on Michael's hand, giving him a small squeeze.

The car navigated in concentrated quiet for several minutes. Tori watched out the window attentively. She outwardly wore her placid disguise, although the lack of knowledge wore on her nerves. Noticing the sign as they crossed into New Jersey, she began to feel a heightened amount of curiosity, *what the hell is going on?*

Michael had perked up as well, peering out his own window more keenly as the landmarks were becoming all too familiar. Passing a sign that read *Short Hills*, Eli finally began to explain. "We brought you here so that you can help us assess a situation, at the request of the victims." He twisted in the seat and spoke to the man seated behind him.

Michael muttered, "Oh, shit," under his breath and studied his wife's profile carefully as Eli continued, Tori focused on the man who spoke.

"Two days ago, the home of your former employers was vandalized, and several of the staff murdered. For some reason, these men think *you* will be able to help with this investigation. So, here you are." His voice sounded cross, as if he were suppressing his negative commentary on the decision to bring Michael in.

Tori inwardly breathed a sigh of relief, as this really had nothing to do with her, and she was only there for the moral support of her companion. Meeting his gaze, she managed a weak smile of reassurance, noting the tense lines that marred his handsome features.

The car pulled through a large pair of wrought iron gates

and onto a large estate, making its way around the curving drive to park in front of the massive home. The sun bright in the late afternoon, Tori continued to gaze about with great interest.

Using their German for privacy, Michael commenced to give her the rundown on what he knew. "This is one of the houses *Indelible* owns, one that they all share. They have individual residences, but this one they bought together for times when they were working in New York, which is fairly often."

His eyes peering around more rapidly, he continued, "The estate is roughly eleven acres and the house has seven bedrooms or suites, each with a private bath, walk in closet and sitting area, plus a whole assortment of other community rooms. It's a fucking palace. Theirs is a real *rags to riches* kind of story, if you get what I mean, and this is their showplace."

After taking his summary in, Tori nodded. "What were your security details like?" she probed, causing Michael to swing his head around to look at her. "Sorry, old habit," she shrugged off the question with a sheepish smile.

"We only kept a few security personnel here at the house," he returned her grin, *I'd be more shocked if she didn't ask*, "And the gate is or was manned twenty-four-seven. One inside on the cameras. Two that patrolled the house and grounds. Pretty light. No idea if they had changed any of that, though."

The car rolled up in front of the entrance, and Eli got out. Opening the door for the couple to exit, Michael climbed out and Tori slid across the seat to look up at the enormous structure. "How many square feet?" she paused to inquire.

"Just over nineteen-thousand, all told," he replied, grasping her fingers once more as they made their way up the short flight of steps and inside.

Smiling, Tori noticed he seemed to be holding onto her more than normal as they reached the doorway; *that or I'm holding onto him.*

Inside, the spectacular entry brought the house to life. The main staircase came down right into the foyer of the great hall, the floor made of a bright and cheerful checkerboard pattern laminate. There were large living areas off to both the left and right, and a hallway that went down the left side of the staircase, leading farther back into the house.

Immediately, Tori noticed that many of items she could see were smashed and broken, which gave her a chill, a small house in Scottsville, Texas, coming to mind. *Relax baby girl, just some punks trashing the rich guy's house*, she tried to calm her jittery nerves.

To the left of the front door stood a table, where the pair dropped their packs on the floor underneath. Turning to Eli, they waited to be given a rundown on what was going on, but he remained tight-lipped, only motioning for them to follow.

Trailing behind him, they were led down the narrow hall. They weaved through several other rooms and passages before arriving at a very large kitchen on the backside of the dwelling. Upon entering, Tori could see all four of the band members scattered around the room. Michael entered first, releasing her for the moment, quickly met by a warm welcome.

"Thank God you came, man," Brian Madson pounced over to him, slapping his hand in a hearty shake.

"No worries, man," Michael nodded, "I'm gonna do whatever I can to help get to the bottom of this."

The rest of the group eagerly echoed his sentiments, and Tori felt a little out of place as she surveyed the opulent design and listened to their familiar, manly banter. *Yeah, I can sure see the riches.* Stepping out from behind her husband to have a look around, the guys made their first realization she was present.

"Hey, you found your girl," Cody Pierce, their lead singer commented, surprised to see her.

The girl he spoke of did not respond, lost in thought as the group of men carried on around her. Moving towards the far wall, she could see the wide yard, filled with various shades of lush green and bright floral splashes. Beneath the window, the wall had been painted with thick splotches of black spray paint. *Well, this don't look good.*

She could hear the men talking, and suspected they were discussing her, distantly registering her name had been mentioned. She had become too engrossed in the odd things she had seen to worry about socializing at that particular moment, and paid no attention to the aimless chatter.

Michael noted her absorbed state, taking the opportunity to show off his wedding band, "Yeah, Tori's my wife, not just my girl." He grinned broadly at his former employers, a group of men he had come to think of as friends.

The four men congratulated him, although they were not as enthusiastic as he would have hoped. He recalled that Brian, the guitarist of the group, actually had a strong dislike of the girl. *Probably a bit of rivalry there,* Michael surmised, *but then again, Tori's pretty good, so it's justified.*

Furthermore, he knew Collin, the bass player, had offered to add her to his list of female conquests. She had turned him down, which surely didn't sit well with the man. This only brought him a sense of deep satisfaction, having won the prize for himself.

Getting back on task, the men began to share details about the incident. Tori, taking up a squatting position, intended to have a closer look at the graffiti under the window, as something appeared to be showing through from underneath. She reached up and began to flake off bits of the paint.

Noticing her intrusion, Brian intercepted her with a small punch on the shoulder, "Hey, don't touch anything," while giving her an angry scowl. "You don't even belong here."

Well, he seems as fond of me as ever, she noted with a grimace. She blinked up at him for a moment, "I'm only trying to help." *I guess he's right though; it's Michael they wanted, not me.*

Rising, she pursed her lips while Eli admonished her with a small, irritated wave of his hand, "Just... stay out of the way." He spoke in French, and his use of their once private language disheartened her further in light of how things had turned out between them.

Shoving her hands into her pockets in a disgusted manner, she did her best to comply. Sufficing herself to visual investigation, she glared at the spot from a short distance instead, as if concentrating would reveal what lay beneath the dark smudges.

A few minutes later, the group led Michael on a tour to survey the damage, as it appeared to be random, with only parts of the house being affected. Hanging back as the men, followed by Agent Founder, exited the room, Tori dropped to her knees beneath the window, again picking at the flecks of ebony paint. *There's something lighter underneath... why paint on the wall and then cover it?*

A sick feeling washed over her as one of the covered symbols held a familiar shape. *No fucking way. Gotta be a coincidence.* Her heart pounding, Tori got to her feet, eager to rejoin the group before they missed her.

Exiting the kitchen, she scurried down the hall. *The last thing I want is to have Eli come looking for me.* She had no desire to talk with the man alone, convinced no good would come from such an encounter. Following the voices through the maze, she continued to see marks that had been left on various walls along with the smashed furniture and decorations that had her stomach tightening into a series of knots.

Recalling her thoughts from their plane ride, she felt odd that Michael had once worked in the house, and she reminded herself the connection had actually been the Dragons. It had been a few months since he had explained to her how and why he had taken the job with the band. Trying to remember the details, she knew that Eddie had instructed him to apply for the position.

Reaching a room at the end of a hall with no other exits, she realized she had made a wrong turn and would have to backtrack. *Damn it. Dead end.*

Her thoughts continued as she retraced her steps. *Basically, his job was intended to allow him access to Brian, on a personal and full time basis. Why?* Continuing her tally of what she knew, she deduced that the position had been the reason her husband had ridden with the group of outlaws that raised her; he wanted to earn the assignment.

And, it was an odd job in itself, as Eddie never cared about anyone personally; so his being sent here had to be business. His motives for the move were unclear at best, leaving her with little to ease her mind, or convince her that the two facts were not related.

It could still be a bunch of punks... but Eli said staff members were murdered. Vandals don't usually take it that far, or attack places that are guarded. Hearing the voices growing stronger, she observed that the house itself was indeed immense.

No wonder these guys seemed so spoiled when I first met them. In essence, they were rich beyond caring what other people thought of them. *This is only one of their properties, and it strongly evidences that they have enough money to do or buy whatever they want.* For a moment, she almost felt sorry for them, being separated from normal everyday people in that way.

Confident she had caught up to the group, Tori considered if their assets could have been a possible motive for the attack. *It does seem likely, as a lot of this stuff they tore up seems expensive. As it is, we have to rule out this other possibility before I go making suggestions as to the culprits. Unless I get some real, concrete proof, I would just look like a crazy woman.*

She started to make a sharp right turn into a study, and then hung back for a moment, noticing more paint beneath another window across from the door frame. Turning away from the dark splotch and peeking around inside the small office as she entered, her blood turned to ice in her veins.

Someplace Safe

The group had made their way into the tiny workplace ahead of Tori, and were busy discussing a message painted on the white wall behind the smashed desk. The letters were crooked, but easy to decipher - *WHERE'S OUR BITCH?* - surrounded by a plethora of graffiti and markings. Michael had inquired about it, and the group was running through the growing list of female persons they were personally involved with that could be the intended reference.

Her breath growing shallow, Tori could see that everything had been destroyed in the room, or so it appeared from the door. Cautiously making her way further in, still staring at the message, her mind ran in a chaotic loop. Arriving in front of the smashed writing table, she noticed a doorway on the left hand wall that led into an adjacent room.

To the right of the doorway stood a tall, wooden bookcase, and this had not been touched. The hairs on the back of her neck had begun to prickle as she felt drawn to the crowded shelves, inching her way closer, and realizing that the items were intact.

Stopping in front of the collection of photographs and

memorabilia, her breath slowed to a deep pant, *oh my God, it's a shrine.* The items were all rather old, and there were photographs of a family, consisting of a mixture of a man, woman and two children featured in all of them.

A large picture of the young girl with long dark hair and blue eyes sat smiling at eye level, with a good sized stuffed bear sitting next to it. She frowned at the brown plush toy, *he looks familiar... but missing something... a ribbon for his neck?* She resisted the urge to touch the matted fur and could feel her hands begin to tremble as she asked timidly, "Who're these people?"

"Hey, don't *touch* any of that. God damn." She could tell Brian felt more than annoyed as he snapped, "That's my family, and it's all I have left of them."

Michael cleared his throat in reaction to his tone but said nothing, aware of the man's protective sensitivity of his past.

Tori turned to look at the collection's owner squarely. He had dropped his gaze to his feet. Drawing a deep breath and releasing it slowly, he struggled to keep his manner even. "They died, when I was a kid. I'm sorry; I know you didn't mean anything by it." Brian gave a failed attempt at a smile, the stress of everything happening around him leaving him feeling raw. *Fucking bitch; God, why is she even here?*

"In a car," Tori stammered, and he looked up from the shoes he had been inspecting.

Running his right hand through his near black hair he reluctantly agreed, "Yeah, in a car accident."

Tori could feel her heart pound as she pushed for more, "In a car that burned."

At this, Brian's head snapped to face her, and he only nodded for a moment, then gushed in anger once more, "How the hell did you know my family burned to death in a car?" *No one knows that shit!*

Tori fell into full on panic, her palms stinging as she

clenched her fists, nails digging into the flesh. Shifting her eyes quickly up and down the shelf, then across the desk to the message on the wall, she bolted around. Grabbing Eli by the front of his shirt, she slammed him against the empty space on the left side of the door frame. She held him pinned easily, being at least five inches shorter than her and very slight in build.

Not to alarm the others until the time came, she chose to use their French to curse him, "Why the fuck did you bring us here?" glaring in wait of his response.

Eli stared at her blankly, "I have no idea what you're talking about." He remained flat calm and allowed her to grip him without a struggle, but had chosen to maintain the conversation as privately as possible.

Michael moved to cut in, "Easy, love; we don't wanna go assaulting the federal officer," *even if he is a piece of shit,* he added to himself.

"What the hell is going on here?" Brian joined the conversation, also in the foreign tongue.

Hearing his words, Tori froze, absently releasing the man she had been clutching. "You speak French?" she asked in bewilderment, returning the conversation to English.

"Yeah, of course, my whole family did. My mother was from Quebec."

Tori stared at him for a full ten seconds, her mind racing, trying to fit all the pieces into place. Licking her upper lip anxiously, she began to make demands, "You," she poked Eli in the chest, "Get them out of here. *Now.*" Towering over him, she wasn't going to take *no* for an answer.

His anger reaching boiling point, Eli fought back. "Look, I don't know who the fuck you think you are, but you're in no position to be making demands." His face grew flushed as he spoke, and Tori realized she had never seen him angry before.

Cutting him off, she spoke in a condescending tone. "You don't get it, huh? Well, let me spell it out for you." Her arms flailed about her as she punctuated her explanation. "*Michael* was their bodyguard because *Eddie* sent him here. To watch this guy."

Tori swung her hand to indicate Brian Madson. "This," she held her arms up and twirled in a slow circle to indicate the area around her, "This is a trap, and you brought me right into it." She did her best to remain in control, the adrenaline coursing through her body.

"A trap?" Eli began to laugh, "And have you forgotten that Eddie is *dead*? I wouldn't have thought so... since *you're* the one who killed him," he taunted her, perhaps trying to make her look foolish.

"No, you stupid prick," Tori clenched her jaw as she bit the words at him and spun around, snatching a black marker off of what remained of the desk. Climbing over the rubble to reach the graffiti covered wall, "*This...* is a scorpion." She drew a box around one of the symbols that surrounded the message, "It's Brett Spears' mark; *leader* of the Scorpions - the man who offered Eddie three hundred thousand to *buy* me from him before I killed him."

She moved back to the bookcase, panting and waiting for her words to sink in as she studied the contents of the shelves more closely. The smirk disappeared slowly from Eli's face, and he shifted his gaze to Michael, "Is that true? Did Eddie Farrell send you here?"

Michael gave him a small nod, "Yeah, he did." He admitted the fact while shifting nervously as he looked over at his former employers.

"So who the hell is Eddie Farrell?" Brian demanded with upturned palms.

Michael started to explain, but Tori cut him off. "We have no time for this. We are in *deep shit*." She slapped her open left palm with the side of her right, as if to chop it, "You've gotta get all four of these guys outta here, right now! You gotta take them somewhere away from here… and away from me. A place not associated with any of them in any way…" Her voice trailed off as she spoke, her hands moving about her in desperation.

Turning around anxiously in a type of bouncing motion, Tori folded her hands in front of her face, "I warned you. I warned you this would happen and that they would pay the price for what I've done." Looking over at Eli, the tears formed in her eyes as she begged, "Please, get them out of here."

He almost asked what it was worth to her, but catching himself, he looked back at Michael and decided to hold his tongue.

Brian, still confused, made one last attempt to get a straight answer out of someone. "Why… are these scorpion guys… coming… after me? What the hell do they want?"

Drawing a deep breath, Tori felt defeated. Shifting her gaze towards him, she tried to break it to him gently. "Me," she chirped softly. Reaching over, she gave the picture of the young girl with the bright smile a tap with her knuckle, "*This*… is me."

It was Brian's turn to laugh.

"Oh my God, you're claiming to be my sister? Well, I got news for you honey; you're not gonna get your hands on me or my fortune that way." Stopping abruptly, he looked over at Michael, his brow furrowed deeply, "Are you in on this? You are, aren't you! Is this what the two o' you've been up to? Trying to figure out how to get your clutches on what we have?"

He used his hand to waft around, indicating the band members and their luxurious house. His eyes darted back and forth between the couple, his tone full of venom.

Michael remained calm, only blinking at the man. *Surely this asshole remembers I'm here because he requested me.*

Brian ranted on, "Well it ain't gonna work, 'cause she's *dead*. She died and she's buried next to our parents. That's the other people in the pictures." Brian's voice changed, beginning to sound strained as he pointed at the shelves. His face had become drawn into a grimace, and Tori knew he didn't believe her, and why should he?

She studied him for a moment, her mind still a muddle of conflicting thoughts and ideas. She wanted him to be safe, as she knew what could happen to him. She wanted the Scorpions to be dealt with, and she knew how hard that would be. Faced with those facts, she knew what she had to do. Turning to Eli, she commanded, "I want my weapons back."

Eli stared at her. "You know I can't do that," he spoke as if he were talking to a child.

Surging towards him, she hissed loudly, "*You* don't have a choice. You either hand 'em over, or I'm gonna show you what I can do with just my bare hands." Her face flushed, and he could see the veins in her neck as she threatened him with bodily harm. Reaching inside his jacket, he produced the pistol and knife that he had confiscated from her that morning in Texas.

Taking the knife from him first, Tori gave the button a push, allowing the blade to pop out the end. Giving it a quick inspection, she closed it with the same action and bent over to tuck it inside her boot. Standing straight again, she took the .9-mm pistol from him. Dropping the clip out to inspect it as well, she spoke to Michael in their covert language.

"Get them out of here. Please. Take them someplace safe." She lifted the back of her jacket and placed the pistol into the waistline of her pants in the small of her back and straightened herself.

"Where are *you* going?" Michael countered.

Pausing, Tori allowed herself to look down at his lips, then brought her gaze back to his eyes; "Hunting." Leaning forwards, she kissed him with a quick peck on the lips, and he reached to catch her arm and hold her there for an instant.

"I'll take them to our place," he told her, still in German, "Come home when you can. We'll be waiting."

Tori gave him a solid nod and headed for the door, Eli trailing along behind. He didn't understand what they had said, but it didn't matter. She was leaving, and he had a strong feeling she was finally going to take care of that job they had been needing for her to do.

Time to Hide

Michael watched as his wife exited the room, an uneasy feeling churning in his gut. Spinning the ring on his left hand with his thumb, he knew they may have had all the time together they were ever going to get. Pulling himself back to the situation at hand, he straightened himself and began to bark orders.

"All right, we need to get the hell out of here. You guys go get two changes of clothes and throw them in a bag. Nothing flashy. And grab whatever cash is lying around as well. You got five minutes." He held up two fingers, talking to all four members of *Indelible*, who stood staring at him as if he were sprouting extra limbs. At their failure to respond, he tried again, "Look, you guys wanted me to come here, and I'm here. Get your asses movin'!"

The four men exchanged glances and began to talk amongst themselves as they left the room and made their way upstairs, giving the impression they were going to comply. Michael followed them in an effort to speed their progress. He had no desire to come face to face with the Scorpions, should they return, and getting the guys to a secure location was his priority.

Cody threw his items into a dark grey gym bag, muttering to himself the entire time. Exiting his bedroom, he found Michael in the hall and decided to have his say. "Why exactly are we leaving? Because that crazy girl, who you married, thinks she's Brian's sister?"

Michael gave him a lengthy stare, his expression unreadable, waiting for the others to join them.

It took closer to twenty minutes for everyone to assemble, but eventually they were ready to depart. Leading them down through the warren of rooms and hallways, Michael headed up the group, looking around the house at the various individuals who were dispersed throughout the building, collecting evidence and poking around. He knew it would be foolish for the Scorpions to attack them there, but as soon as they were out, it would become more dangerous.

Stopping in the lobby, Michael asked in a monotone voice, "Is your plane where we can get to it?"

Studying his former employee, something about his flat calm had begun to unnerve Brian. Michael had been their head bodyguard for over four years, and damn good at what he did. Any danger they had ever faced had been addressed with the cold, calculated stillness he saw before him, and he considered how the threat could be very real.

"Sure," he nodded, "Do we need to fire it up and have it ready?"

"Yeah," Michael agreed, "Have them prepare for our arrival and file a flight plan for your place in Florida. We'll travel by other means from there."

Moving to comply, Brian disappeared into one of the side rooms, leaving the remaining three band members standing in awkward silence. None of them really understood what was going on, but having developed a deep trust of the man who gave them orders, they did not dare question him further. Besides, their newest head of security had been murdered, so where else were they going to turn?

When Brian returned, he informed them he had also called for their car, and it should be around front momentarily. Wanting to be sure they would have everything they needed, Michael went down the checklist again: clothes, phones, chargers, and cash.

"Meh, we can pull cash out or use our credit cards," Chuck interjected dubiously, not seeing the significance of their situation.

Shaking his head, Michael stipulated they would not be using any plastic once they left the airport. *You don't know it guys, but you're about to disappear.*

"When we get where we're going, we'll be taken care of, so bring what you have and it'll be enough," he explained, thinking about the small town and the people who had accepted the couple so readily. They would be in good cover once they got there, and he had enough money in the bank, they could hide for a long time if they had to. *Longer than these four spoiled men could probably handle.*

Michael pulled his bag from under the table, where it sat alone. Heading out the front door, the group climbed into the long black car and shifted into their seats, the strain thick in the air. Running long fingers through his nearly black pelt, Brian finally demanded, "You really think that girl is my sister? I mean, how the hell would that be possible? She was in the car with my parents." His voice held deep emotion, and they could see he was riding on an emotional roller coaster; "We buried her."

Michael bobbed his head in understanding, but having met the Dragons and Eddie Farrell, he knew nothing was ever what it seemed. Taking a moment to choose the precise words, "There may have been a little girl's body in the car, but if Eddie wanted her, you can bet he had devised a plan to cover his tracks. The only way to know for sure would be to have you tested. I can make a call… see what we can do to get the ball rolling… keep it quiet too, if you want."

Brian slowly nodded his agreement. "Yeah, we gotta know, one way or the other." He looked out the window, still too unnerved to contemplate what the impact of any results might be.

Borrowing Cody's cell, Michael retrieved Terral Huffman's card from his wallet and called the store in LA to enlist the help of the former federal agent. He gave Terry a brief explanation of what had transpired and what he needed. "You think you can help us get him tested without having too many people know?" he finally asked.

"Sure," Terry quickly agreed, "You'll need to have his blood drawn in Florida and sent over to an FBI branch. I'll take care of making the contacts from here and get the results to you when they come in, no problem."

"We really appreciate that, and we'll have it there as soon as we're able."

"No worries. Tell Tori we miss her," Terry's voice grew quieter at the sentimental thought.

"Sure thing, you know she misses all of you, too."

Hanging up the device, he gave Brian a small smile, and explained how they were going to get the blood sample submitted and it would all be taken care of, "And I'd like to hear your story; how your family died. Maybe once we're on the plane. I know it may not be easy to talk about, but it'll really help to get a fix on our situation."

Michael had been curious about Tori's true identity for many months. Confident her origins had finally been found, he held his excitement in check, eager to find out all he could about the accident that had ended the family's lives and set her history in motion.

Brian only nodded. Chewing his knuckle, he kept an eye

out the window as they rolled along, his mind turning feverishly. *Son of a bitch. This is gonna make things pretty fucking awkward if it turns out to be true. Michael my brother-in-law and Tori my sister. There's some good news.*

Exiting the car at the airport, the group made their way through the crowded terminal and quickly passed through security. A few of the airport team joined them as they made their way, weaving through the tunnels inside the back areas of the labyrinth until they came out in a small area for private planes, where they climbed the stairs to board their Citation X. Skipping up the steps, Michael could feel himself relax at the almost routine activity, realizing he had actually enjoyed some parts of his old job.

Their plane not as luxurious as some private jets, the guys had always preferred to do their partying on the ground. It served its purpose, quite comfortable for the few hours the group spent in flights from place to place when the need arose.

Taking their seats, Chuck and Cody moved to the back group of chairs, taking the pair that faced the front of the craft. Collin and Brian took the next set of two forward facing with two empties behind them that faced the back of the plane.

Michael sat in a rear facing seat in the front so he could see all of the men as they traveled. Surveying them as they fastened their seatbelts for the taxi onto the runway, he smiled to himself. *Well, they seem to be taking this sudden turn of events in stride.*

By the time the plane had leveled out, Brian had gathered his memories, and prepared to recount what had happened to his family. "It was summer," he began, "And it was late June. My parents had driven me to visit my grandparents for a few weeks of my vacation. Nikki had just turned five in May and would be starting school in the fall." He appeared tense, wringing his hands repeatedly.

Michael nodded, "Nikki is your sister?"

"Yeah," Brian confirmed, "She was," he paused for several minutes, staring out the small portal to his right while he considered his words. Finally, his eyes shifting nervously, he confessed, "Ok, look. I had a lot of guilt about her dying when I was a kid. She followed me around incessantly when we were little. I could never get rid of her and she was annoying as fuck. I mean, she never shut up. Always talking and asking questions."

"I was ten that summer and all I wanted was to get away from her," he angrily defended his actions to the group. "So when she wanted to stay too, I threw a fit. It was *my* vacation, not hers."

Michael watched his Adam's apple bob as he swallowed before he finished the thought, his voice trailing away by the end. "If I had allowed her to stay, she wouldn't have been in that car when the accident happened. Basically… it was my fault she died." The small space grew eerily silent, as that had been part of the story his band mates had never heard.

Michael could see the pain etched in his face. Trying to put him at ease, he shook his head slightly, "That may not be true. It may be the fact she was in the car that the accident took place." Brian gave him a startled look, which Michael waved off, "We can talk about that later. For now, you can go on."

Brian nodded, inhaling deeply and allowing the air to release noisily through his nostrils. "We got the call that night. The police came and asked a lot of questions, as I wasn't in the car and that seemed to raise some suspicions; at least at first."

"Apparently, they had stopped at a café to eat on the way home… and there were several people who recalled seeing them as it was right before the accident. Now, knowing my sister, she was pouting or giving them grief because she hadn't gotten her way. She was a spoiled brat and pulled that crap a lot."

Pausing, he rubbed his hands together, still obviously tense, "Anyways, they left the diner, and sometime after that the car crashed and burned. I mean burned to the ground, all three of them inside of it. The only thing that survived was her teddy bear, which you probably saw on the shelf in my office."

"How did the toy survive?" Michael interrupted him, "If the car burned completely?"

"How should I know?" Brian shrugged, "They found it on the ground at the scene. That's all I can tell you; that, and I had to convince them to let me have it, because they investigated the crash for several months before it was deemed an accident. We buried them together in a small cemetery there close to my grandparents and I lived with them until they both passed away about ten years ago. I still own the property. I lease it to a family who runs the farm."

The group sat for several minutes, quietly digesting his story. Michael ran his fingers tensely through his sandy curls as he recalled Tori's description of her nightmares. *Yeah, she talked about a diner in her dream... and she described the car, engulfed in flames.* He felt certain she was this man's sister, believed to be dead. He realized this meant some other family's little girl had been buried next to Tori and Brian's parents.

It also meant no one would ever have located her through missing children records. *Hell, no one was even looking for her as she was already thought to be dead.* Eyeing his newly found brother-in-law, he knew this would be a struggle to come to terms with, for everyone. *Damn, Eddie was a smart son of a bitch.*

Shortly thereafter, the plane landed at MIA. Exiting the

craft, the group discussed their arrival at Brian's beach front property, when Michael interrupted their conversation sternly, "We aren't going to the house here. We're just trying to cover our tracks a bit." Leading them out of the terminal, the group took a minivan taxi to a bus terminal and bought tickets to a smaller town in northern Florida.

The guys became confused but followed him on instinct. He had been amazing at his job of protecting them in the past and they trusted him whole-heartedly. Climbing onto the bus, the group spread out and didn't bother to talk, each man left to consider what had taken place and how this would affect their future if they were forced into hiding for very long.

Four days later, they arrived at the tiny house and shop in Texas. Looking around the quaint apartment that Tori had decorated, a strange feeling came over Brian, and he considered what it would mean if she were really Nikki, back from the dead. They had made a stop at a lab to have his blood drawn in Florida, and he had been anxious to get the results ever since.

Finding her guitar in the closet of the smaller bedroom, he brought it out with the intention of playing it. Seeing Michael's icy stare at the notion, he thought better of it and placed it in its tiny stand in the corner. *Man, this really sucks*, he muttered to himself. He had claimed the couch as his part of the accommodations and flopped down there in utter disgust.

Ghost of the Past

Eli followed Tori as she left the group standing in the small study. The couple had dropped their packs by the front door as they entered, and she paused there long enough to split the money tucked inside Michael's bag, taking about twenty thousand for herself. Lifting her own pack onto her shoulder, she made her way down the hall to exit out the back door and through the extensive back yard.

Aware that Eli still followed her, she stopped next to a group of trees, swinging around to confront him. "I want some God damned answers!" She kept her rage under control, but barely so. "How long have you known that man was my brother?"

He ran his fingers through his dark hair, blue eyes swimming as they avoided meeting hers. "Listen," he chose his options carefully. "We had been investigating the Dragons, among other groups, for a long time. We had no idea how they were all really connected until you were found and shed some light on things. Edward and Gerald Farrell were part of the original investigation. Now, all of that information is classified and I really can't go into details with you."

Tori's gaze grew stone cold, but she didn't interrupt as he pushed on.

"We really didn't know about your family or where you came from. And, I hate to say it was convenient, but it was decided it was better if you remained, shall we say, disconnected, from your past life. There were lots of unanswered questions and we needed you to fill in the blanks."

Shifting his gaze to the ground beneath them, Eli looked uncomfortable, confessing how he had used her. "I really felt bad about the way things turned out. Honestly, you meant a great deal to me, but by the end I got the feeling I was the one being played. You seemed so happy to move on to LA, like I really meant nothing to you. And now you're married to Michael, and that just makes it even worse. Like I was easy to forget."

Her expression softened at seeing his features drawn in pain. "It wasn't that easy," she muttered quietly.

Eli's eyes meeting hers, he knew he had her. Daring to touch her, he looped a few fingers of his right hand with her left, avoiding the cold metal of her wedding band. Leaning slightly towards her, he relished in her scent, his mind flooded with memories of her, sunshine, and singing birds.

"So," he huffed after a lengthy pause, "What's our next move?"

Tori swung her gaze around the lush garden and sighed deeply. "There's really only one thing we can do." She knew they were pressed for time, and the list of workable options short. In truth, she wasn't happy about where that placed her in the mix of things. Dropping his digits and indicating for him to follow, she made her way to the back gate to let herself out onto the side street.

Eli trotted eagerly alongside her as she explained she

would have to locate the Scorpions and get into the midst of them. "It's the only way I'll be able to get close enough to take them out." She glanced over at the man next to her, daring him to object.

He made no such attempt, only questioning her going into the group alone. "I mean, it's going to be dangerous. I could get another agent to go in with you, under cover."

Tori shook her head, knowing that would never work. *A Fed would be smelled out in short order.* She needed someone else. Someone who knew the rules and could play the part and, unfortunately, she knew just the person for the job.

"Leave it to me," she reassured him. "Please make sure the guys are taken care of; that's what I need you to do." Quickening her pace, she dismissed him with a wave of her hand. With Eli taking his leave, Tori made her way to a bus stop and caught a ride to the Millburn Railway Station.

Purchasing a ticket to Baltimore, she located a small shop and acquired a padded envelope with postage to ship it. Seeing the selection of cellphones, she also picked out a small white go-phone. Back outside, she slipped her ring inside the package and penned a brief note - *Keep this safe for me, Love Tori.* Her heart heavy, she held it for several minutes before dropping it into the large blue box. Once she had taken care of her ring, she activated the phone and made her way to catch her train.

Finding the entrance, Tori pushed her way through the crowded Amtrak platform, where people waited for the transport that would continue on into Washington after she had arrived at her destination. She took up a spot against the wall, partially protected by one of the pillars so she could keep an eye out around her.

Slipping her hand into her pocket, she fidgeted with the smooth edges of the phone while trying to decide what she would say. *He isn't going to like this*, she mumbled to herself repeatedly.

When the train arrived, she made her way onboard along with the rest of the hoard and fortunately found an empty seat next to the window. Plunking down, she forced a heavy breath from her lungs in an agitated manner, peering out at the people milling around below.

Tori pulled her backpack around to her lap and sat holding it, ready for the trip to begin. Dejected, she toyed with her finger that once held her wedding band. It felt odd, with the shiny metal no longer encircling it. The train pulled away from the platform and she removed the small device from her pocket, studying it for a few minutes before retrieving the pink slip of paper from her wallet.

Nervously, she punched the number into the small keypad and waited to hear the ring. After four pulses, she feared he might not answer, when a male voice picked up the line, "Bueno?" Tori's heart thumped heavily in her chest.

Faltering, "Hello, Enrique?" Not hearing a response she tried again, making good use of her Spanish abilities, "Enrique, it's me, Tori."

This time, the man replied, clearly stunned to hear her voice, "Oh my God! Tori, is that really you?"

A weak smile formed as she airily replied, "Yeah, baby; it's me."

"What happened? Where are you? Are you ok?" He didn't give her time to answer anything between his rapid-fire of questions.

"I'm fine baby," she soothed, "Really. But I'm in a bit of a bind and could really use your help."

Enrique didn't hesitate, eager for them to meet. "Where you at, baby girl? I'm in Florida, but I can head out right now."

"That's very good, actually, I think Charlotte would be a

good spot. Let me call you back when I get an ETA." Ending the call, she didn't feel any more relaxed, and clutched her pack while she considered how things were possibly going to turn out. One, she knew that Enrique would want an explanation, which she felt reluctant to share all of the details with him if she could help it.

Two, he would be expecting her to service him while they were together. The thought of lying with him troubled her, even with the removal of Michael's message. However, it was a moot point, as she would have to be willing to perform when they found the Scorpions if she were to have any hope of convincing them she wished to join them. She exhaled a deep sigh as she considered the tangled web she prepared to weave; that and the price the story would cost her.

Her thoughts briefly drifted to her husband and newfound brother. Quickly pushing them away, she reminded herself sternly, *thinking about either of them right now is a waste of time. You have a job to do, baby girl; you'll have to focus if you ever want to see either of them again.* Combing her fingers through her dark waves, she stifled the urge to cry.

Arriving at the next station, Tori exited the train long enough to purchase a new ticket for North Carolina. Discovering that she only had ten minutes until departure, she ran to make the connection. Falling into the seat on her new vehicle, she again wished she had some idea how Michael was doing with getting *Indelible* moved towards their home.

Her head pressed into the seat, she allowed herself to think about her mate for a few minutes, recalling how she had permitted him to stay with her when they arrived in Texas. It had been against her better judgment, but she had allowed her heart to guide her the night he had begged her to agree.

"I'm not ready to leave," his words haunted her. He reminded her so much of Henry and she had been powerless to refuse him. The scene had replayed itself too many times to count in their few short months together. *I'll be home as soon as I can*, she promised him silently into the darkness.

With a cleansing sigh, she chose to stow her bag this time. The ride would be nine hours and she hoped to get some sleep. Giving Enrique a quick call, she told him she would arrive at 4:00 am, a nervous grin crossing her lips when he responded in a sultry tone, "I'll be waiting."

He actually sounded excited; if he still has feelings for me, this could get very complicated. Staring out of the window, her mind worked in circles as she considered how much of the truth she would be able to share with him. She needed to clarify her feelings for the tall, dark man; someone she had once thought she loved. *I can't let my heart make too many of the decisions; it's my brains that'll save us.*

Forming the basis of her plan, she rationalized how she had always been a fairly honest person, only taking the time to outright lie if there were a clear benefit to doing so. Of course, she also understood if Enrique knew the truth, he might not be willing to help her, and then where would she be? In the end, she couldn't make up her mind, and fell asleep while still considering the path she should take.

Tori awoke several hours later, as the train stopped in Charlotte. Grabbing her bag, she made her way out the exit to find he indeed waited for her on the platform. She had not been sure what she would say, but he did not wait for any explanations. Walking straight up to her, he swept her off her feet, swinging her into their customary playful circle, her arms instantly wrapping around his neck to hang on.

Placing her back on the ground, they held the embrace, resting their foreheads against one another as he stroked the line of her back. Tori stood still, allowing him to fawn over her for a moment, and then pushed her face towards his to bring their mouths together.

Enrique parted his lips and the kiss deepened into more than a friendly hello. She knew he was getting the wrong idea. Choosing to not set him straight, she freed her lips and whispered hoarsely, "Do we have a room?"

"No, but we will," he replied with a grin.

Taking her hand, he led her out of the station. The couple swung onto the back of his bike, Tori looping her arms around him to massage his chest as they rode. She liked the feel of the vibration on her female parts, allowing it to excite her, preparing to play the part of lover to the best of her ability.

Enrique didn't take long to choose a motel, and they made their way to the room without delay. From inside his bag, he pulled out a few items; surprises for her.

She wasn't shocked to see the tube of gel appear as that would be a given knowing him like she did. She welcomed the other item more, as he had stopped to purchase a rather large bottle of Smirnoff Silver, and went to find the glasses as she kicked off her boots and jacket. Staring at it, she realized it had been a long time since she had tasted even a drop. *He even remembered my favorite brand.*

"I's really surprised to get your call," he said in a cheerful tone, "You know, after alls this time."

Nonchalantly examining the bottle, Tori tried to share in the small talk. "Oh, well, things have suddenly gone crazy on me and I really need your help. But that's not what I want to do or talk about tonight..." She allowed her sentence to hang as she gave him her best *fuck me* pose. She had never been one to lie, but she wasn't above using her body to get what she wanted, and right then it was the only card she had to play.

Pouring the glasses, he gave her a wicked grin, "Yeah,

it's been too long," obviously eager to get down to business.

However, if she thought it would be easy, she had been mistaken. Her hand reached for the glass, but stopped short, and her fingers began to tremble uncontrollably. Unable to force them to grasp the offering, Tori curled her digits into a fist before pulling them back.

Looking up into his dark brown eyes, she licked her upper lip, her mouth suddenly dry. She drew a deep breath as the emotion washed over her. She became conscious of the fact she could not be with him unless he knew the truth. She searched for the right words, and he could see the pain drawing lines on her face.

Deciding to end her suffering, he confessed quietly, "I knows about that guy you been with."

Startled, her expression shifted as she demanded, "What're you talking about?"

He sat the bottle down and moved to stroke her arms with his palms to soothe her. "I seen you, in a little town in Texas, three months ago, or so. There was some guy with you, in this little garage, and I sat and watched you, trying to decide what to do. I seen the two of you together, and I realized, you didn't need me anymore. That's why your call surprised me."

Turning slightly away from him and staring at the floor, Tori considered whether he was lying or not. That long ago, she and Michael weren't really together, as they had only been married ten weeks. But then again, she couldn't be sure. "And what did you do about it?" she asked calmly, still facing the dresser and avoiding his stare.

Enrique shrugged, "I hung around for a few days, watchin'. Then he must've spotted me, 'cause he came down to the diner to sees me. Told me you guys were together. I mean, I hadn't actually seen him touching you or you kissin' him or anything, but he said you was with him." Tori's jaw dropped slightly. "Anyways, from your reaction, I guess things must've hit a rough spot."

She could not stifle a laugh, "A rough spot, that's a good one." She shifted her stance, trying to collect herself. He still half held her, and her eyes moved timidly up to his face. *He's so handsome, and if he doesn't love me, he puts on a good show.* Swallowing hard, she whispered in a trembling voice, "They found my family, Enrique. My brother. They tore up his house to get to me."

He could feel the air hang in his chest, refusing to come out. Staring into her wide blue orbs, he heard himself reply in an equally low tone, "The Scorpions? Is he Ok?"

She nodded, "Michael has taken him to hide while I go after the group responsible."

Enrique looked stricken. "What do you mean, *go after* the group?"

She could hear the concern in his voice, and knew she needed to confess her plan. "I'm gonna kill them," she stated flatly, glaring at his lips as she raised her chin in defiance.

Enrique stared at her, his head shaking slightly in disbelief. "You can't be serious." His rising voice strained, and he gripped her biceps roughly, turning her to face him squarely once again.

Placing her hand on his chest, she tried to calm him. "Remember what Eddie taught me? The way that he raised me, to be his secret weapon? I won't be safe, and my family won't be safe, until they're eliminated."

"Yeah, I agree, but you can't kills those guys. There's eleven of them if they haven't replaced me, and after alls this time, I'm pretty sure they have. You're not gonna beat twelve men. Even with my help, we lose here!" Enrique could feel the stab of pain in his chest as he acknowledged the fact that he still loved her; the thought of anything happening to her petrified him.

Her gaze flitting between his deep brown eyes and his

curved lips, she replied softly, "I don't have a choice. I have to try, and if I lose, at least they won't have a reason to go after the people I care about anymore." Her expression bleak, she spoke with conviction, waiting for him to comprehend; to see things her way.

Catching a whiff of loose hair, he smoothed it, carefully contemplating what she had said. "So, what's the plan?" he managed.

Her relief evident on her face, she explained with a hint of excitement in her voice, "We have two ways of approaching them. Either way, I'm gonna need your help locating the group. After that, I can go after them alone and hope to get lucky. Or, I can ride in with you and we can pretend we're looking to join back up with them. Either way, it'll be a risk, but if we go with the second option, you'll be in danger as well."

"I don't cares about that. I'd rather gos with you and be there to help if I can." He didn't even flinch at the possibility of being harmed or killed if it meant her odds were better. Leaning forward, he kissed her, allowing his lips to slide gently over hers, then nuzzle her cheek. "I still love you," he whispered into her hair, lacing his fingers through it and against the back of her head. They stood for several minutes, him clinging to her in earnest.

Feeling her rigid stance, he picked up on the elusive vibe she emitted. Eventually, he gave her some room. "So, you and that guy're serious about each other? I mean, you're really with him?" Enrique felt sure he would regret the answer, but he had to know where he stood before they moved to the next step.

Her voice quivered, "He's my husband. He gave me his name." She essentially avoided her own feelings on the subject, and let it go at that.

Enrique released her to turn his back, trying to hide the

pain that coursed through him. Even though he had left her with Michael by choice, it still hurt. "Does he know where you are? That you're here with me?"

"No," she replied swiftly, "I mailed my ring back to him with a note to keep it for me. I didn't tell him my plan... but he's a smart man. I'm sure he'll know why."

Lifting his face and turning enough to look at her, he acknowledged what an incredible woman she was, and how much she would be willing to sacrifice for the people she loved. "You knows what you're gonna have to do. If you wanna convince them, you're gonna have to play the part."

"I know. I played the part for a long time, and I can do it again. Have to do it again. As long as you know it's just an act, then we're good. When this is over, I'm going home."

Shifting to shove his hands in his pockets, he nodded, "Yeah, I gets it." *She's gonna fuck me, but she don't want me.* Looking at her squarely, he rolled his tongue for a moment as he mulled over her words, *we'll sees about that.*

Staring down at the glass of liquor, Tori willed herself to swallow it. She knew it would help her focus and do what must be done. Her right hand moving quickly, she lifted the glass and gulped the liquid, her mind briefly flashing David Long, the camp around them as he trained her how to drink. Closing her eyes as it went down, she prayed that Michael would forgive her.

Like Old Times

Enrique moved to shut off all the lights, save a small bedside lamp, which cast a soft warm glow across the room. She watched him, summoning all the emotion within her while she helped herself to a second glass of courage, preparing for their encounter. The realization she would give herself to him, and many others over the next few weeks swirled in her mind.

She knew she would not be their victim. Not this time. Not even when she allowed them to hurt her. *I've been had by men too many times. It's time for me to take... to take what I want and to use it... to twist it, and to make it my own.*

When he reached her, he kissed her deeply, measuring her state of drunkenness. He discovered her eagerness, as she returned his intimate caresses, grasping him in the near dark and tugging at his clothes. *She really wants me,* his excitement spiked within him, *she can lie to herself, but she can't lie to me.* "Oh my God, baby girl... you know I missed you so bad..."

"Shut up and fuck me," she cut him off, commanding his obedience - and his silence. She wasn't there to make love to him. "And make it dirty," she clutched a fistful of his dark hair as she pressed her body firmly against his, eyes boring into his lips, "Really dirty, baby… you know I like it that way."

Enrique grinned at her offer, knowing she did indeed like it that way. Primed to obey, he removed her clothing roughly, breathing against her flesh and biting as he went. In the process, he noted the tattoo that had been peeking at him from between her breasts and down her shirt.

Inspecting the new mark closely, he saw that it held Michael's name etched in the shadowy edges; not glaringly obvious, but noticeable when you faced her, looking at the spot. A knowing smirk crossed his lips as he considered the man from the diner. *Yeah, it's time to give her what she really needs.*

He kissed her deeply, loving the way she responded to him. His fingers explored the soft curves of her body, and he ran his palms coarsely over her flesh. Allowing her own hands to move over his and help him undress, she enjoyed the contour of his muscles and the desire they stirred within her. *I want this*, she persuaded herself; *I want this badly.*

Getting on her knees, she took to the job of pleasing him without hesitation. Her lip soon tingled, and she chewed it without thinking, growing eager and driven by desire. Pulling her up, their kisses pressed their mouths together almost painfully, the taste of him awakening the old feelings she had hoped she had forgotten.

Turning her away from him, he pushed her across the small round table, pressing her husband's name into the grain of the wood. He brushed her hair off to the side so he could enjoy the full line of her back, running his hand the length of her spine. She relaxed into his demanding movements, and he determined her level of wetness before sliding himself easily inside of her warm hollow. Teasing her soft folds with short strokes, his fingers stretched her with the gel.

He presumed he had been the last man to take her that way, part of him wanted to be gentle, but at the moment, his thoughts were becoming lost, clouded by raw need. Once she could take two fingers easily, he shifted his position and pressed his way inside. She moaned loudly beneath him, grasping the edge, unwilling to complain. She focused completely on maintaining her façade.

Feeling her tense with the action, Enrique leaned over her naked back, his nipples touching her bare skin through the hair on his chest. *You're mine now...my bitch... and you can forget about everything else.* She excited him beyond words, and he had to focus not to lose himself too quickly.

Forgetting the things they had talked about, he continued to work her. Need driving him, he slammed against her, moving deeper within her fervently as he pulled her hair, wanting to hurt her, just to see if she would scream for him. *God, it's been so long.*

Grasping at her flesh, he felt her tremble beneath him. *She really loves this*, his thoughts swirled, *and she's mine! Fuck that bastard, and Brett. When this is over, I'm gonna keep her. I swear to God, I'm gonna keep her.* Lacing her fingers with his own, he whispered roughly, "You're so dirty, *my* baby girl," breathing heavier and pushing harder against her.

Filling her fully, he pressed her against the table, waiting for the urge to pass so he could continue. Lying still, he recalled all the times he had been with her, loving the way she always accepted him, compliant if not zealous. Feeling the need subside, he took forceful movements once again, and she began to moan more deeply. His right hand squeezed her fingers, his left sliding smoothly up and down her supple skin and enjoying the firmness of her toned body.

Holding himself off a second time, he felt the urge to

drive her even harder, and she began to make louder grunts along with her deep groans, her left hand still gripping the edge of the table. He clutched the skin along her ribs, squeezing it tightly as his thoughts ran wild. He could hear himself smacking against her wet folds of skin, thinking how his roughness excited her, her noises the stuff of thrilled exhilaration. *So nasty, baby girl... such a filthy little bitch. God, I love that about you.*

Squeezing and pushing, beyond holding any longer, he released with loud gasps and a few jerky thrusts. Leaning over to rest against her, his chest heaving, sweat dripped from him to mingle with hers, and he knew he had become lost in fucking her; his drug, the root of his addiction.

My God, we could do this every day; I have to keep her... I have to find a way. Nuzzling the back of her ear, he whispered to her, his hand tugging on large sections of her long dark hair. She panted heavily beneath him, clenching her jaw and releasing it repeatedly.

Holding his position until finally forced out of her, he stroked her damp skin. Allowing himself to slide out, he pulled her up with her arms, and they stood together for several minutes. He reached around to stroke the line of her front, then curled his arms around her from behind in a tight embrace, allowing his hands to say what she did not want to hear. *I need you, baby girl; I need you so fucking bad.*

When they parted, he noticed the streaks of blood, visible in the low light. She assured him it couldn't be helped, and then kissed him deeply. Her skin on fire and longing for more, her enthusiasm had not been completely unfounded. Leading him to the bathroom, they stepped into the tiled cubicle together, and she washed him. The touch of her hands and cajoling of her fingers revived him quickly.

Pushing to turn her, he pinned her to the wall with her chest and belly pressed against the flat surface as he made his way inside her once more. Most of the gel washed away, it stung her as he moved, despite her inebriated state. She breathed deeply, willing herself to accept him. She could feel her warm folds ache, and he slid his hand around her hip to cup her mound of flesh. Applying pressure, he used it to gain leverage as she pushed back against him.

She forced her palm flat against the wall to hold herself steady, and he drove into her almost angrily as the spray of water splashed across their nakedness. She emitted louder noises beneath the cascade, demanding that he continue, "God, don't stop, baby... for the love of *God*, don't make me beg..."

After several minutes, he felt the waves of ecstasy overtake him and he surged against her once more, exhaling deeply as he clutched her wet naked skin. *My God, she's so good at this*, he breathed against the back of her head.

Noting she still wobbled somewhat from the liquor, he made sure they were both clean, and wrapped her in a towel after exiting the steamy stall. Moving back into the room, they stretched out on the bed, and she lay on her belly, her mind clouded by the drink, still feeling restless in the haze.

Enrique ran his hands across her smooth skin until sleep fell over her. Holding her in the darkness, he confessed in a whisper, "I love you, baby girl," keenly aware she had never spoken those words to him.

It made him feel odd that she hadn't, and he considered the possibility that she was really playing him, and had been since he met her. *It's so hard to tell.* He had known her a long time, and seen her play this game too many times, with too many men. *She makes lying look so easy.* Lost in thought, he too drifted off to sleep.

The next morning, she awoke to the feel of fingers prying their way inside her; Enrique preparing his favorite hiding place for another round. She relaxed into the motion, and he took her without question or comment. Still groggy, Tori felt the conflict inside her chest, as she yielded to his desire.

She appeared hungry for the encounter, the sensation thrilling to her, and she breathed deeply as she accepted him. Pulling up on her hips, he straddled her to change his angle, making it different from what she had been accustomed. Gripping the blankets tightly, she relaxed, eager to be his nasty girl.

You like this... you want this, she told herself repeatedly while breathing heavily through an open mouth, not quite sure if it were a command, or an admission. Satisfied, they showered again, and he caressed and squeezed her bare flesh, claiming her as his own.

Dressed, they made their way out to find lunch, where he continued to touch her at will. Finding an open air café, Enrique felt transfixed by her in the warm glow of the sun. He placed his chair only a few inches away from hers, to kiss and pet her continually, loving the feel of her long dark strands as he pulled them gently through relaxed fingers, and grinning broadly all the while. He leaned his forehead against her from time to time, waiting for their food and languishing in their familiarity as he cooed in her ear.

She had applied the makeup that covered her scar, and he became aware how other men around them noticed her. *No wonder Eddie marked her; traveling with her like this would attract way too much attention.* He was already growing possessive of his new toy, having wanted her for more years than he cared to admit. He could not wait to get her back to their room so that he could satisfy himself again, grinning at her lustily while they ate in comfortable silence.

Seated next to him, Tori appeared much harder to read, being more practiced at hiding her emotions. Watching everything that moved around her, she did not look happy or sad. She stared out of her pale blue eyes, wearing her typical stoic expression. No smile, no frown, completely blank and indecipherable as to any inner thought or sentiment.

Seeing this, Enrique missed how happy she had been in LA. She had never said that she loved him, but he had always assumed that she did, at least back then. Now, he wasn't so sure. Reaching over, he dropped his arm across her shoulders and stroked her firmly, longing to hold her and sway to the sound of a jukebox as he had done in the tiny bar the first time she had been his. Leaning into the crook of his arm, she emitted a small sigh, which only left more questions in his troubled mind.

Walking back to the room a few minutes later, she allowed him to hold her hand, a stab of guilt panging her briefly as she considered that she wasn't playing fair, by permitting the acts of intimacy. *You're one cold hearted bitch,* she admitted to herself in disgust. *These things are beyond what's necessary to get the job done. They also will undoubtedly stir feelings in him that would be better left at rest.* Stealing a sideways glance, she briefly compared herself to Eli, and his deceitful ways, before she pushed the thoughts aside and refocused on her current project.

But, I do like having his strength to surround me; it comforts me. She could at least admit that to herself, having learned it was ok to need things from other people. She knew she would not be alone in her endeavors with him by her side. Selfish as her actions were, she could not bring herself to push him away. *I own this*, she reminded herself, *and I own him,* she recognized with an inward smile. *If he gets hurt, it'll be a small price in the end.*

Reaching their destination, they made their way inside for another session of dirty sex. She had rationalized their lustful acts, thus far, as necessary to the task at hand, and felt compelled to take her new-found strength even further. This time, she instructed Enrique to sit in one of the chairs and she placed herself on top of him, taking him into her soft folds, and driving herself against him while he prepared her.

When ready, she took him into the new position as she had done in the tiny bar in LA the last time they were together. The action electrified her, with her solely in control; it felt like old times, and she smiled as she focused on what she did to him, pushing the reasons *why* out of her mind.

Enrique could see the hunger in her eyes, her own need unmasked. Cold sober, she had not bothered to take any more of the Silver that sat on the counter, and she stared into his eyes as she took him. This left the man no doubt that she was, in fact, enjoying their activities. *She really loves this*, he deduced, *I dunno why she pretends that she doesn't, hiding her needs and desires, torturing herself that way.*

After they were satiated, Tori slipped into the bathroom for a long and private cleansing under the steaming torrent. She stood beneath the warm flow, allowing it to pelt the top of her head, as she thought about the things she had already done. Of course, there would be more to come, even darker acts, as the job would require her most depraved self to be unleashed. She refused to think of what she did as right or wrong. *It's too late for that. You'll do what must be done,* not seeing any other choice.

Allowing her fingers to glide across her breasts and then down to her delicate lumps of flesh, she noted they had become swollen from their vigorous activities. Touching herself, the mere thought of this excited her, and she could feel herself already becoming torn between the two men and the different ways that they thrilled her. Leaning against the wall, she stood with the water flowing over her, her mind blank, too tired to consider her situation any further.

Outside, Enrique opened his phone, ready to make the call that would set things in motion. He would've loved to spend an entire week with her, just having scx, but he knew there were other lives at stake. Besides, he could not be greedy with what wasn't really his, even if he hoped to claim her in the end.

"This better be good," Brett answered the call gruffly, "We've left you be, what the fuck 're you botherin' us for?"

Enrique smoothed his hair, "Yeah, well, I'm only calling 'cause Tori asked me to. She wants to meet up with you guys. I think she misses her old life."

Brett laughed heartily; "Got my message did she?"

Enrique feigned ignorance, "I dunno any details. Only that I gave her my number an' told her to calls me if she ever needed me. She called, and this's what she needed." He paused for effect then continued as persuasively as he could muster, "She really wants a position in the group. She's ready to work for us, right? We should alls let bygones be bygones. I'm ready, an' I think she's ready too. If you'll haves us."

Brett seemed to consider the offer carefully before he replied, "Take 'er to the camp in Ohio. We'll meet ya there tomorrow night." Flipping the device shut, Enrique listened to the water through the door, contemplating the girl who stood beneath the shower.

Their plan daring, their position would be precarious. He would have to hold his tongue, and he knew they would test her loyalty well before they accepted her into the group. *This is gonna hurt... for both of us,* he thought as he entered the bathroom to join her in the thick fog of the tiny room.

Hidden Places

They had only been at the house two days when Michael received a small brown envelope in the mail. Using his pocket knife, he cut the end open and allowed the object to slide out onto his open palm, deeply saddened to discover it held her ring.

Finding the small slip of paper hidden inside, he read her brief note several times, then placed it in his wallet to stare at in private. He placed the ring back in the grey felt bag, back into his pocket to carry with him like he used to before he had given it to her.

After its arrival, he slept little and worried a lot, struggling not to think about what she was doing or who she was with. *I know she sent it back to me for a reason; whether to hide that she's mine... or to ease her conscience at what she must do.*

But she had asked him to keep it for her, and that gave him hope that she would come back to him when she could. Besides, he had other things to worry about, and more pressing matters to keep him occupied, as the caretaker of the four men who needed protecting.

The next morning, Michael had decided to allow Brian to play Tori's guitar, and informed him as they ate in the tiny kitchen. Her brother appeared eager, having missed his own and the release that music brought him.

Michael smiled at the familiar sound, and noticed how similarly they moved when they held it, but his tone wasn't quite the same as hers. *I bet it's only 'cause I love her that makes her better*. After a bit more deliberation, he made his way down the narrow hall to retrieve her spiral of songs from the place she kept her special books.

Sliding the top drawer of her dresser out, he only glanced briefly at the other contents, scowling at the small book of German fairy tales. He had read the message penned inside it once before, and it only made him angry to think about it. *He wrote it that way on purpose, not saying he loved her, but giving her enough to keep her hoping. Sorry bastard.* He wished his wife would discard it, but at the same time, he understood why she couldn't.

"Here," he made the offer in a curt, subdued tone, having returned to the living room, notebook of thoughts, memories and dreams in hand.

"What's this?" Brian snapped as he stared up at him, still not fully in control of his feelings at the situation.

"It's Tori's music. Her book of songs. Maybe it'll help the two of you bridge the twenty years you've been apart."

"You seem pretty confident." Brian mocked him, grasping the frayed pages, "I mean, we ain't even got the results of your little test back. What if I'm not who you think I am?" he studied the other man keenly, not wanting to invade the girl's private thoughts too hastily.

With a deep sigh, Michael avoided his gaze by staring out the front window of their living room and watching her tree sway in the hot afternoon sun. "I heard your story before. The one about the day your parents died. She told me about the car that burned. *'Like a house burns,'* she said. And she knew about the diner. I can't see her having made it up." He shook his head, still avoiding his glare, "You don't have to look if you don't want to. Wait for the results."

His shoulders drooped while heading out to the garage, Michael went to piddle with the bike he had started tearing down. It felt odd, working on motorcycles without his wife to watch over him. *I love her so much. What am I gonna do if she don't make it back?* Quickly pushing the thoughts from his mind, he refused to wander down that path. *She's coming back,* he repeated, refusing to see it any other way.

The rest of the small group of men fell about the town, doing their best to entertain themselves by hanging out at the café or in the garage. Chuck and Cody both had bike experience and liked to play around with Tori's tools, but Michael noticed right away their hands were not nearly as practiced as hers had been. He allowed them to handle her favorite things with a clenched jaw as she would probably have preferred that they didn't.

Right away, the group convinced him to buy a television and they sat for hours staring at the device, watching movies they picked up at a store in the next town. They also had discovered the local pub, and enjoyed going there in the evenings to drink. They seemed to be accepting their confinement in relative discomfort, keeping as many of their old habits as they were able.

Thinking about their lifestyle, Michael wished they wouldn't chase the local girls. They were lying low, and being recognized could have serious consequences down the road. However, the men had appetites, and felt they were justified in satisfying them. Shaking his head, he recalled how easily men like them got what they wanted from the females around them, and from life in general. *Good luck getting them to listen to reason,* he quibbled mentally.

They had been living like that for over a week, when a black four-door sedan arrived, driven by Warren La Buff. He paid them the visit to deliver the results of Brian's DNA testing.

Michael and Brian sat with him in the small living room, allowing him to take the couch while they each stood or sat in kitchen chairs facing him, both stirring in anxious motion. They were nervous, the impact of this news on Tori's future, as well as their own, heavy in the air.

Warren had a brown envelope with him, and once the three of them were settled into their seats he opened it and withdrew a small stack of papers. Taking a few minutes, he explained how the DNA test looks for markers, or matches that indicate that two people are genetically related. He further explained that there are essentially two kinds of DNA, the kind found in cell nuclei, the brains of a cell, and that found in mitochondria, or the tiny energy producing parts of a cell.

Nuclear DNA comes from both parents while mitochondrial DNA comes from the mother, and is less altered as it passes from mother to child. This DNA was a perfect match between the two of them, which meant they had the same mother. Furthermore, the nuclear DNA indicated that the two of them were in fact siblings, most likely sharing the same father.

Brian sat stunned for several minutes. Michael had jumped up at hearing the news and walked around his living room and kitchen, running his fingers through his sandy brown waves, trying to take it all in.

Contemplating their next course of action, he glowered at the man seated on his sofa. *Warren La Buff seems friendlier than she described him. I wonder if he'll help us put things right.* Retaking his seat, he began to question the man on her behalf.

"So, when do we get her emancipation nullified?" he demanded in a quiet tone.

Warren only stared at him, blinking in return.

Michael pushed the issue with a pointed finger, "You guys had her declared a minor and given a birthdate so that she's only sixteen years old. Obviously, if she's this girl, Nichole Peters, she's actually twenty-five years old. We want that fixed."

La Buff hem and hawed, "The committee will reconvene at a later time to decide how to handle the situation."

Recovered from his shock, Brian felt he had a vested interest in the proceedings as well and burst into the conversation, "Did you give her a lawyer when you did all that shit? Or get a second medical opinion?" his voice dripped with accusation, his brow wrinkled with concern. Warren looked surprised for a moment but said nothing. Turning to Michael, he continued, "No worries, man. We'll get this shit straightened out, big time."

Brian had only had a few days to consider his sister being alive, but knowing for sure, he wanted to take care of her the best he could. She had been a nuisance to him when they were kids, but his feelings of guilt over her presumed death had made him quite ready to accept her being alive as a second chance to make things right.

"And what about the other girl?" he continued with his assault on their visitor. "The one they buried next to my parents. She came from somewhere. How're you guys gonna find out who she is?"

Looking him up and down, Michael grew impressed; the man had obviously been giving more thought to the situation than he realized.

Warren surrendered a small nod. "We will be exhuming the body and doing our best to identify it. She is more than likely a child that was abducted the morning of your family's accident in a nearby town, killed and placed inside the car to take the place of your sister."

Michael sat giving him an icy stare, beyond angry. *This man's obviously as cold and calculating as my wife described him.* "I bet you are."

The words escaped him, but he showed no emotion as Warren turned towards him sharply, barking in a stern voice, "Listen here. You have no idea how much we have been dealing with," trying to justify their actions with a pointed finger. "There are many aspects to this investigation that I am not at liberty to discuss with you. Lots of lives at stake here, and not just these four fools." He wafted his hand towards Brian as an indicator of who he referred to.

"We've been working this case a long time, and we have no intention of losing our hold on it over one girl, sixteen or twenty-five. In the end, she is of no consequence. The needs of the many outweigh the needs of the one, especially her. She is a murdering whore. That's it. End of story." Rising, La Buff headed for the door, leaving the two stunned men to ponder what he had said without looking back.

Heart of the Matter

The couple rode into the rally point the next afternoon, their minds fully focused. The stakes were high, and one misstep could cost both their lives. Brett had instructed Enrique to take her to their camp in Ohio, and they had checked out of the motel to head out as soon as they were dressed from their shower. Only stopping to nap in an all-night dive for a couple of hours, they were right on schedule.

Riding through the trees on the narrow dirt road, Tori took note of how the feel of the area was similar to the camp where she had grown up. She had never been there before, and she grew curious to see how the second group kept themselves. Wending their way into the forest itself on a rocky trail, she knew that as a dark and out of the way location, bodies hidden here might never be found. She shuddered to think how many the place more than likely held.

Pulling up in front of the cabin itself, she saw that it appeared to be very unlike the small structure that had occupied the center of the Brazilian bush camp. There were a couple of tables in the clearing in front of the oversized cabin. Having a look inside the lodge used by the Scorpions, the much larger room included bunks along the left hand side for sleeping, fifteen in all.

There were four picnic style tables set in the center, and a large fireplace on the right, with a wood burning cook stove and group of cabinets on the far end. Tori felt quite impressed with what she saw. *They have electricity and even running water.* She could not help thinking it indicated that the Scorpions were soft. *Of course, the climate of Ohio is very different from that of my Amazonian home, which is something to consider before I judge them sight unseen.*

Making her way back outside, Enrique gave her a quick overview of the camp's layout, pointing out the area they used as a firing range, along with the personal facilities, and a few other landmarks. Saving the gun range for later, she cut a path through the trees to explore the rest of the immediate woods around them.

Working her way in a circle, she found several trails and locations that could be useful when they were ready to put their plans into action, including the small shed that housed their generator a few hundred feet from the cabin. She also found the small set of metal pipes that formed the bars they used for physical exercise, which meant they at least kept themselves in shape.

The final surprise, she came across the beat up '54 Ford truck parked inside a run-down shed. *So this is how they keep themselves stocked so far from real civilization.* The path back up into the camp took over an hour to navigate, so she knew they had to be self-sufficient somehow.

Completing the loop, she made her way back to the main structure. Enrique sat leaning in a chair next to the front door, enjoying the late afternoon sun. Walking up to him she asked, almost annoyed, "So, where are they?"

He gave her a shrug, "We beat them here, obviously, but

I'm sure they'll get here quick as they can." He gave her a knowing grin while looking her up and down, then dropping the chair on all fours, slid his arm around her waist. Their bodies pressed together tightly, he ran his hands firmly over her backside and gave it a playful squeeze, lost in the feel of her.

Tori looped her arms around his neck, leaning in to share a kiss, becoming lightheaded for a moment as they mingled. In the distance, the roar of motorcycles broke the stillness of the forest, so there probably wasn't time for them to have a romp before the rest of the group arrived, and she found herself disappointed by that fact. *Might as well get what we can,* she lazily continued their foreplay.

Taking a deep breath, she inwardly prepared for her re-acquaintance with the crew, while her hands followed the line of muscles beneath her fingertips. *I'm fully primed to play the role of willing recruit,* she reminded herself.

Several times, she had mentally gone over what most certainly would take place once they were reunited. Although she could not remember a great deal about the group, she fully expected them to be very similar to the Dragons in structure and form.

The time she had spent with Enrique would hopefully have conditioned her for being the entertainment once again, and she felt ready to perform for the group of men. She also expected to experience some violent episodes related to that, confident Red had not been the only man to have such a fetish, feeling the need to inflict pain while performing sexual acts.

Yeah, I got this covered... they're gonna fuck me... and they're gonna beat me... and I'm gonna milk it for all it's worth. She closed her eyes as Enrique continued to stroke her, his hands finding the warm flesh beneath her shirt and pushing up until he could toy with her nipples. Her panties were growing moist, despite her mind not being fully into their heavy petting, and she heard herself moan as he caressed her.

Still mentally going over details of her situation, Tori also expected to be tested, perhaps similarly to what the Feds had put her through at the hospital. *Only this time it'll be for physical knowledge, such as weapons and techniques.* But then again, they may not care about her being part of the team and simply want her around for physical satisfaction. *This seems unlikely knowing the sum Brett had been willing to part with to get me. I wonder if he already knows what I can do?*

Seeing the glimmer of chrome through the trees, she considered the possibility of also being beaten as a way of testing her loyalty. Enrique had also noticed the metal, and reluctantly removed his hands from her, mentally preparing himself as well. *Damn. Just a little longer and I could have had her to myself one more time. I should'a made it quick.*

Allowing a deep sigh to escape her lips, she straightened her clothing, and could feel her muscles tense when the string of bikes rolled into the clearing. She did not relish the idea, but considered that she would have to endure all forms of being dominated. Steeling her reserve, she repeated her mantra. *Chin up, baby girl; you can do this,* remembering to stifle the smile their making out had left on her lips.

Observing them all before her, Tori had no clue who any of them were, save Brett and Buck. They were the leader and his second, the rest not being worth ever learning their names. Taking a quick head count, she noted there were, in fact, twelve men on wheels, so Enrique had been replaced. It disgusted her slightly that she had no clue which one was the new guy, but it couldn't be helped.

Making her way over to Brett as he killed the engine and swung off the seat, she held her placid expression the best she could, having a difficult time keeping her smirk at bay. He offered her his hand and she gave him the familiar shake, even though she had never been considered a full member by anyone outside the Dragons; the price of being a woman.

He grinned at her broadly after he gave her a quick half hug and slap on the back. "You look really good with that makeup on," he tossed at her jovially, shaking his red curls lightly. "Guess you was gettin' soft, your brother bein' rich an' all."

Tori didn't bite, standing still and blinking at the man blankly. She knew he would test her, and she had thought she would take his beating in stride. However, when he made his move, her instincts kicked in and she could not bring herself to go down without a fight.

Countering his opening swing, she twirled his arm away from her and punched him in the ribs, knocking him back a few steps. Dropping her jacket to the ground, and her pistol on top of it, the fight became a sparring match.

As the ring of onlookers formed around them, each of them landed some punches while they sized each other up. Tori considered what might happen if she bested him, and Tony's old advice came screaming into mind, *"You can't beat us all."* He had been talking about the Dragons of course, but the same principle applied here. That's one reason the groups were structured as they were, as a functional unit.

Perceiving another man moving to step in, Tori laid down the hammer on the interloper. Knocking him to the ground, she roughed him up a bit, not realizing he was the man she had wanted to kill the first time they saw her in Florida.

Dan only wanted a little retribution, now that he held the position of surprise aggressor, but it didn't work out for him this time any better than the last. After she put him on his back, she knelt on his chest with her knee to pin him while she beat him about the ears and face until Brett called out, "Tha's enough."

Obeying his orders as she would have Eddie or Red, Tori stood and looked at her new owner, awaiting the next command.

Brett beamed again, walking over to the girl who stood about two inches taller than himself. *God damn, she's quite a prize.* Putting his hand on her waist, he followed the path down to her round posterior and pulled her hard against him in the same fashion Enrique had done. His fingers tickled her in private places, and she played along as she had done with Eddie many times, allowing his touch to stimulate her, glad that her companion had prepared her for what comes next.

Tori's heart began to pound as he tugged at her jeans to undress her, and she continued to do her part by kissing him and offering to help. Within a few minutes, she stood naked, wishing she had been able to down her customary beverage before their arrival, as it was now too late.

She would have to take part in the night's activities and maybe even make it look like she had enjoyed it while sober, as she still wasn't sure how she would play this. With nimble fingers, she helped him get his own pants open and bring out his little friend before he laid her back on the table behind them.

To her surprise, he laid her face up, taking her soft folds so he could look her in the eye while he fucked her. He wasn't a large man, but she faked her enthusiasm for him well, lifting her legs and grasping at him firmly. He didn't take long to finish himself, excited by her eagerness to be with him. Not backing away, he stood panting for a moment as he lay over her, toying with her breasts and examining her new tat that covered Eddie's old mark.

"Who's Michael?" he asked directly, his finger tracing the outline of the rose.

She had known that would happen. "The angle I was workin' when I was so rudely interrupted by the Feds. They showed up an' dragged me to New York so I could meet my brother." She looked him in the eye as she spit out the half-truth.

"Feds, huh," he ran his palm over her bare skin, and then leaned in to kiss her again.

Tori slid her hand up to the nape of his neck, massaging the hairline as she moaned at his caresses, her legs wrapped to hold him against her.

Breaking it off, he whispered hoarsely, "Eddie always said you was a crafty li'l bitch." Pulling away from her, he gave a single order, "Don't kill 'er," zipping his pants as he headed into the cabin.

Tori felt her heart stop as she realized what he had done. Lying still, she didn't even bother trying to resist. She had been there before, and she knew the only way to win; give them what they wanted.

The first one to her gripped her thighs and rolled her over onto her belly. Already naked, it only took a moment for Buck to pop his pants open and yank himself out. Trying to insert himself into his preferred location, he seemed to not like it as well as he had the last time he had been with her. Settling for her soft folds, he drove against her angrily for a few minutes. However, someone had come prepared, and she was soon greased and ready for him to take what he really wanted.

Off to the side, Enrique watched and waited, planning to be the last to make his way over to her. When his turn came, she still lay face down on the table, but she had blood on her skin in places, most certainly in pain. It gave him an odd feeling, the roughness of their sex somehow different from what the group did to her, and it angered him slightly that they had touched her, even though he had known he would have to share.

Not to draw attention, he opened his own jeans, but it took a bit of effort to make his way inside her. The sun had set, and her skin felt clammy, so he removed his shirt, laying his bare chest against her flesh to warm her. He then slid himself into her warm chasm, and laced the fingers of her right hand with his. She whimpered softly as he stroked the back of her head with his free hand.

Moving slowly, he tried to give the impression he was just one of the guys having his turn, but on the inside he felt deeply concerned. "Baby girl?" he nudged her softly as she lay breathing in shallow puffs beneath him. *Oh my God, what if they really hurt her?*

Taking a ragged breath, she whispered, "I'm ok, baby; do what you gotta do. Don't blow this," and gave his hand a squeeze.

A wave of relief washed over him as he nudged her affectionately. *She's just playing along... clever girl,* he praised her, the realization of the depth of his feelings for her, intense.

Sliding himself into his favorite position, he took her readily, causing her to gasp and moan quite loudly. He chose to forgo his usual routine, pushing himself to the end in one step. Leaning over as he finished, he mumbled into her hair, "I love you, baby girl." Pulling himself out, he went to clean up and find out about dinner for her.

Enrique being the last, someone dropped a towel on the table next to her, along with a small pot of warmed water and a small cloth to clean herself before she ate. She was not, however, permitted to get dressed, and sat greedily eating her hamburger steak and vegetables while naked. She allowed them to think they were getting the better of her, outwardly cowering with wide eyes and being submissive to whatever whims they fancied.

Inwardly, she watched them, waiting to get to the heart of the matter. She felt confident she would get her chance to kill them as she could already tell they underestimated her. After she had eaten, they led her into the cabin, where a fire burned warmly. Brett indicated for her to sit at one of the tables located inside, and she obeyed.

Towering above her as she perched on one of the benches facing the flames, the grain of the wood leaving a pattern on her unprotected rear end, he demanded to know why she was there. Staring at him, a confused expression wrinkled her face as she stuttered, "You… You wanted me here. You broke into my brother's house and left that message for me."

He squatted down in front of her, poking her left breast on his way by, "An' what about this guy, where does he fit into this?"

"He's Henry's brother," she began timidly. "We met up by accident and he took it upon himself to look after me. It made things easy an' I stayed with him. He's the guy Eddie sent to watch my brother." She paused, adding some tremor to her lip as she spoke, "The Feds came for him 'cause those guys asked them to, an' I went with them. Then I realized the message was for me, an' I came to you." She turned her palms towards the ceiling, hoping she appeared as meek as she currently felt in her bare skin.

"An' you told th' Feds about us," he concluded for her.

Tori gave a shrug and a tear rolled down her right cheek. "They questioned me for months. Put me in a halfway house when they couldn't get what they wanted. Had me declared a minor so they could keep tabs on me. I never gave them anything. No names, nothin'." She shook her head, her lip still trembling as she spoke, and she could see his expression softening.

73

Brett surveyed her undressed curves as she slumped on the bench before him. Eddie had told him things about her the rest of his crew didn't know. He had bragged what she was for, and fucking wasn't it - that was her cover, and he was right… she was damned good at keeping it.

The Scorpions had seen what she did to Dan that first night, seen her fight today, but that was nothing compared to the job Eddie intended for her to do. He wrinkled his forehead as he considered what to do next. Brett knew how and why she had been chosen, that's how he had located her brother. That's also what scared him.

Eddie had chosen her because she was smart. Maybe too smart. "So, what happen' t' th' Dragons?" His tone had become hushed, almost comforting.

Tori continued to allow the tears, pretending their passing had been difficult for her. She had seen the way the people at George's funeral had mourned for him, and did her best to channel their sadness.

"They're dead," she stammered. "I woke up, in a hospital in Chicago. The Feds were questioning me an' told me. If they hadn't found me when they did, I woulda died, too." It had all been true of course, and she only left out the parts that incriminated her.

Enrique stood listening to what she said, and when Brett turned to him, a stab of fear struck her as she realized he might not really be her ally. "Is that true?"

Enrique did not look at her as he nodded, "Yeah, near's I could find out, they still don' know any more than they did."

Tori felt relieved, but she no longer felt sure about her companion. Obviously, there were things he had not shared with her, and she became equally glad she had not confided all in him. *Boy, wouldn't Brett be pissed if he knew the Dragons died by my hand. Thank God Enrique doesn't know!*

Brett considered his words for a moment, looking back

and forth between the two of them. Indicating which bunk belonged to him, he instructed her to go and warm herself inside it.

Scurrying to comply, Tori made her way over to the narrow beds that lined the wall opposite the fireplace. There were five columns, three high, so that the bottom rested barely above the floor, the center positioned at thigh high, and you would have to climb to get into the top, it only far enough below the ceiling to squeeze in. Brett had a center shelf, and she rolled easily into it, wrapping the sleeping bag around her freshly scratched and bruised flesh.

Unwilling to sleep, she lay waiting, listening to the low voices that continued across the room at the hearth, unable to discern what they said. Eventually, Brett came to bed, removing his clothes before he joined her. She discovered her new lover to be less demanding than Eddie or Red, simply sliding in beside her and pulling at her to move on top of him. She eagerly did so, ready to satisfy him as she lay across his toned muscles, looking into his soft green eyes in the dim glow.

Her legs straddling him, she lay against his smooth chest. She noticed he had little hair to speak of, the thin coat barely enough to tease her fingers. He easily slid himself into her warm folds, allowing his hands to take in her soft curves and roam up and down her back.

She moved above him, fucking him with growing intent, kissing the skin along his chin and neck warmly. Pausing occasionally, she kept him from finishing for an extended period of time before she drove him to the end and he clutched at her wildly as he made the noises that indicated he had been more than satisfied.

Continuing to lay next to his nakedness, Tori rested her head on him, stroking his chest with soft fingertips. He seemed to be a different kind of man than those who had raised her; not nearly so cold hearted or brutal. Drifting off to sleep, she almost felt guilty that she would have to kill him, and wondered if there, in fact, might be another way out.

New Marks

Brett had taken a liking to Tori long ago, and having her made him happy, despite the little alarm bells that were ringing in the back of his head. Awakening to find her staring at him, he ran his hand along her jaw, his body eager to have her. She responded to him easily, and would have taken the top again if he had not shifted to pull her beneath him instead.

Sliding between her legs, he found his way inside her wetness, pushing himself in and holding still while he caressed her smooth skin. Running his mouth across her nipples, he liked the way they wrinkled and grew hard, like small pink pyramids that teased his chest as he rubbed against them.

Tori returned his kisses, her hands exploring his back and neckline, pulling gently on his curly waves of red hair. Beginning to push against her, she fell into the role of lover so easily; he suspected he was being played but felt powerless to resist it.

Longing to believe she really wanted him, he squeezed her breasts again as he began to drive her harder. Lifting her feet towards the bunk above them, she grunted noisily, seeming to enjoy the way he felt inside her.

A few minutes later, Brett could no longer contain himself, and grasped at her shoulders, pushing down hard as he finished loudly, his earthy noises resounding in satisfaction. Lying still to deflate within his prize, he nuzzled her neck below her ear, whispering her name. She didn't respond, only lying and panting, accepting his intimate acts calmly.

Satiated, he slid off of her and stood next to the bunk, helping her to make her way out. Several of the others were scattered around, watching and waiting to see if they would once again be given the left-overs. Tori kept her eyes on Brett, uneasy with having to endure another full round of the dirty sex they would demand from her if he did.

Smiling at her, he tried to make light of his group's needs and her ability to fulfill them, "You don't seem too eager to treat them as good as you've treated me."

Tori stared at the floor, knowing he intended to pass her on to them again. Swallowing hard, she replied coyly, "Well, I usually have a little relaxation in liquid form before I make the rounds." Cutting her eyes up at him, her face still downturned, she hoped he gathered her meaning.

Brett only nodded, grabbing his pants and pulling them on, then leading her over to one of the tables, he instructed her to sit, still naked. She could feel his deposit dripping out of her and wetting the bench beneath her as she waited, tickling her as it did.

She could sense the eyes of the group on her, hungrily taking in her soft lines and curves. Moving slowly, she allowed her long tresses to hide, and then reveal her assets in a playful manner. She toyed with them while she could, well aware of what lay in her future, and a sly smile on her lips.

Making his way over to one of the cabinets next to the

stove, Brett opened it and brought out a large partial bottle of rum and a small glass, which he placed before her. Stepping back, he watched in curiosity how much she would consume.

Tori stared at the container for a moment, considering whether or not to actually use the tiny glass, licking her lips in anticipation. *Rum ain't my favorite, but it'll sure as hell do the trick.* She knew she would be ready to perform soon enough.

Pouring the glass full, she downed the entire thing in one long gulp. Looking up at him, her eyes questioning if there was a limit, to which Brett waved his hand in a wafting motion, and reassured in a whispery voice, "Have your fill."

Looking at the puny glass for a moment, Tori pushed it aside and hoisted the bottle, chugging a third of what remained before replacing the cap and calling it good, her arm removing the surplus from her moist lips.

Allowing her to sit for a few minutes, Brett finished getting dressed, and then took the bench across from her. Stroking his chin, "Are you gonna pass out on us?" he queried.

"No," she mentally added the word, *unfortunately*, "I doubt I'll lose consciousness from that small of an amount. Now, if I were to chug the whole bottle," she laughed edgily at her own joke, which made him smile.

He feared that he liked her more than he should have. For a moment, Brett considered not sharing his new toy with the others, but looking around at their anxious faces, he knew that would be a recipe for anarchy. Deciding she was sufficiently inebriated, he stood and headed out the door, leaving the group of men to their own devices.

Tori stared after him as the exit closed, considering how she should respond to the men who were moving closer in anticipation. Rising to her feet, she turned to the one they called Buck, Brett's second in command. "You know," she attempted a conversation, "I can make you feel real good if you let me."

He gave her a wide grin, showing the half of his teeth that still remained in his mouth. "Oh, yur gonna make me feel real good a'ight," he emitted a laugh that made her hair bristle on the back of her neck.

Images of Red flashed in her mind, and she stiffened uncontrollably. Her eyes flitting down to his scraggly teeth, then back up to his steel grey eyes, Tori braced herself.

Buck, a rather large man with his belly hanging over his silver buckle, unfastened and removed it.

She wished she had downed a few more swigs of the vile liquid as she turned, trying to appease the man who seemed hell bent on using his leather strap on her scarred skin, covering it with new, bright red marks.

Tucking her face into her arms, Tori breathed deeply, refusing to allow him to make her cry, and after a few minutes, he judged he had left enough welts on her back and legs. Grabbing her by the arms, he pushed her out flat onto the table, her belly lying against the rough wood, breasts squashed.

Grasping the edge of the table, Tori struggled not to give away any emotion. She had come to learn men who enjoyed inflicting pain took satisfaction in seeing it on her face and hearing it in the noises that she made, and she had no real desire to bring him pleasure. Lying with her face pressed against the table, she closed her eyes and breathed deeply. She had played this game enough times, she knew what to do.

Brett marched with an irritated stomp as he exited the cabin; partly at himself, for giving in to the demands of his crew, and partly at the girl for not being more vocal if she did not want to be shared. *I bet she loves it,* he suspected as he trudged down the trail to the gun range. He had been with her and seen her too many times to convince him otherwise.

That don't matter though, at least she's mine now, and I got her for free. He recalled the bittersweet details of the offer he made to purchase the girl from Eddie Farrell, two years ago best he could recall, $300k being the offered amount. *My entire life's savings, but I woulda gladly traded it for her.*

"I'll even wait for delivery," he had smiled at his old friend encouragingly, "Ya know, 'til after you're finished with 'er an' her job's done." He had felt his blood run cold when Eddie turned to stare at him with his steel grey eyes.

"She ain't for sale, old man. Not now – not ever, I don't give a fuck if you got $300 million. An' where's all yur money at anyways, if that's all you got to offer?" Eddie had sneered at him, disgusted at the way his counterpart ran the Scorpions.

"Oh, ya know, spend a little here and there. It's still a good amount, Eddie. I mean, for a woman tha's a hell of a lot o' cash," he laughed nervously, trying to dispel the tension.

"It ain't shit for *that* woman," he clenched his fists, as if he were deciding if he needed to lay an ass kicking on the man for even suggesting it…

Brett entered the clearing to the range, finding Enrique digging around in one of the gun cabinets. Noting the sour look on his face, he posed a question, "Why ain't you back at the cabin? Not like you to turn down your share o' *that* girl."

Enrique avoided looking at the group's leader, his tone listless, "Not this time."

Brett watched the younger man, analyzing his words, "Ya know, I's really surprised you actually brought 'er to us, 'specially after you took such a beatin' and denyin' ever' minute of it you had no idea where she was."

"Yeah, well, ridin' in here was her idea. I told you, she called me up and asked me to brings her here." Swinging his gaze to meet the leader's glare coolly, "He promised he wouldn't make her bleed."

Brett nodded slightly, "So he said, if he don' get carried away. Ya know how he likes that sort o' thing. Tha's why we make a good team, him and I."

Enrique only nodded, turning back to the case full of munitions, "You gonna test her?" he tried to change the subject. Not wanting his displeasure to become any more exposed, he reached for a rifle and pulled it out to inspect it.

"Yeah, tha's a good one. Le's strip it down, see what she makes o' it." Tossing a sheet on the work bench that shared the awning, he began pulling the gun apart, laying out all of the pieces carefully. "So, if she wants t' be here, why d' ya suppose that is?"

"I think she missed this life. She was with the Dragons a long time. Maybe livin' in a little house and tryin' to play normal ain't for her."

Brett busied his hands with the rifle parts, "Thought you didn' know where she was. Sounds like yur not much of a liar."

"Yeah, wells, I used to be. Not so much now. She broke me, I guess," and he left the conversation at that. Once the items were arranged, Enrique picked up where he left off, "You think she's a witch?"

"Who's a witch?"

"Tori. Like she has powers or some shit. Over me."

Brett looked up at the man across from him, and realized he was serious. Giving him a half shrug, "Why'd you think that?"

"I dunno. It's just that I've wanted her for so long. Since the first time I seen her. And I keep telling myself, I'm gonna fuck her one more time, and then I won't wants her anymore.

But when I'm done, I wants her more than I did before." His own honesty surprised him, and he sat, shoulders hunched, waiting for the laughter. *Real fucking swift... might as well have said you're in love with her.*

Brett only stared at the other man, his own feelings raw in his mind, "I never thought o' it that way." But he knew what his underling meant. "Tha's why I came out here; 'cause I didn' wanna watch 'im beat 'er."

Enrique shifted to stare him square in the face. "You coulda stopped him. You didn' have to lets him, you know." His words were bitter, but he avoided a full-on confrontation.

Brett shook his head, "Naw, it serves a purpose, even if I don' care to watch. We have to be sure o' who she is, what she wants. She's tough, cunning, and manipulative." He grinned, "Her best qualities, come to think of it."

Enrique laughed out loud, unable to deny he had often thought the same thing.

When the group had finished with her, they gave her another bucket of warmed water for cleansing; her clothes and pack returned as well. She kept her face calm as she washed away the blood and body fluids from where they had enjoyed her, taking extra care with the new red cuts that covered her scarred flesh.

Once she was decent and outside, she looked around indifferently, scanning for signs of Enrique. She had been considering the events of the day before, and the time she had spent with him in LA. It had occurred to her, she might have to kill him as well. His absence that morning seemed odd to her, and she didn't dare ask about him. Hearing gunshots over in the area he had indicated as the firing range, she made her way in that direction.

The trail that led to the clearing well defined, her heart

began to thump at a quicker pace as she surveyed their set up. They had a waist high counter where you could stand with your shells and weapons lying on it in front of you, with targets at varying distances down the range.

Turning around from the active position, there stood several gun cabinets under a small awning made of tin. To the left of the storage stood another table, where Enrique stood with Brett, cleaning a rifle that lay in pieces on the sheet that covered the wooden surface. The small amount of rum she had imbibed already wearing off, she blinked at the scene, wondering how far they would go.

Tori had never really liked guns, only considering herself proficient with them after her years of training. A few of the others joined them, curious about the girl they had seen in action only a couple of times. She stepped up to the table, and Brett asked if she knew what kind it was.

She shrugged a reply, "Valmet, M82. Pretty rare."

He gave her an approving grin, and indicated for her to come over to the table at the firing line. Going through various handguns and rifles, he indicated targets he wished for her to hit with the weapons from standing, squatting, and lying positions.

It had been over a year since she had fired a weapon, but her skills were intact and she easily hit the marks he prescribed. The crowd of onlookers slowly expanded as they all wanted to see what mayhem their newest member would be capable of inflicting. Eventually, they grew tired of the guns and moved into hand to hand trials, several of them eager to see how she stacked up against them.

Tori had a calmness about her, complacent to display her abilities. Dan made a third attempt, and she actually began instructing him on his errors that allowed her to beat him so easily. Her voice stern, "No," she commanded, "Do not step in that way."

Grasping his shoulder to position him, she could hear Eddie's voice in her head as he had directed her in much the same manner. *Only back then, when I fucked up, he beat the shit out of me*, which she would never attempt for herself as the teacher.

She quickly realized, this group was not anywhere near the level the Dragons had been. She wasn't sure if soft would be the right word either; *they just seem less effective.* As she worked her way through the gathering, she began to notice the training, or lack of it, this particular team of men held. The Dragons were all ex-military. *Did Eddie put his group together that way on purpose? And if he did, why didn't Brett follow suit?*

She also felt pretty sure she had identified the new guy, as she noticed the young man who kept to the edge, his slight build and wire framed glasses a sharp contrast to the rest of the crew. She would have to ask about when it became safe to do so, as Enrique would know. *But first I'll try to get close to the kid, see if he'll give me the answers.*

Tori took each who stepped up to face her, content to work through them all, learning their strengths and weaknesses and styles of fighting. By the time they returned to the cabin to have a late lunch, she had left no doubt in anyone's mind; she had earned her Dragon mark the same as everyone else.

They had gained a certain respect for her, if not fear, as secretly each knew together they could control her, but one on one, she would likely take the upper hand against most, if not all of them.

Hanging around the cabin, the group reminisced about old times and the Dragons, allowing her to tell stories about them as well. Normally, she would never be permitted to speak in gatherings, not considered an equal to the men. The act had been their way of accepting her, giving her a place among them. Tori outwardly acknowledged the gesture, but inside she knew the move would not distract her from her intentions.

The sun sank low in the sky, and the group turned to more serious items to discuss. Brett had not shared what Eddie and Red had been training the girl for, but the members of the Scorpions had begun to suspect her purpose.

Highly skilled, the girl had clearly been trained, and was more than simple entertainment. Buck pressed the issue, demanding she explain her role within the Dragons, which she remained reluctant to articulate in detail.

With a shrug, she attempted to pacify him, "I did whatever was assigned to me. If Eddie gave the word, I put you in the ground. I cannot say how many it was, or how often. I only know I never missed a mark." She spoke the words matter-of-factly, not intending to brag. He didn't look as if he liked her attitude, moving to impose his dominance over her.

She stood before him, unwilling to cower. His right hand swung and she accepted the open handed slap to the left side of her face, her nose and lip smeared with blood. Straightening herself, she lifted her chin slightly, refusing to wipe at the fresh flow, allowing it to drip from her jaw onto her shirt and the ground below.

Grinning widely, Buck professed, "Eddie al'ays said you's a stubborn li'l bitch." Nodding his approval, "If you *had* killet 'em, you wouldn' admit it, now would ya?"

His deduction startled her, but she did not move, her expression hiding her displeasure at his insight as she blinked calmly at him. Choosing to remain silent, she stared into the stale blue eyes.

He could see her mind turning, and for a moment, he felt his heart skip a beat as it dawned on him: *if I'm right, we brought the wolf int' our midst.*

86

Brett interrupted the scene with a laugh, "Now, why would she kill 'em? She loved those guys, didn'tcha, baby girl?" He smiled at her, not wanting to see any ill in his newfound companion.

Still looking dead into Buck's cold stare, she replied flatly, "Yeah, I did. They were my family."

Set Things Straight

True to his word, Brian contacted his attorney as soon as Warren La Buff left the house. Explaining how his sister had been discovered, and then laying out the details of how she had been moved to LA to be declared a minor and emancipated, he inquired how the situation could be challenged.

Robert Frost, Attorney at Law, laughed out loud when he heard the insanity of his new case. Reassuring his client they would set things right, he hung up the phone to give Special Agent James Godfry a call. It had been some years since he had had a client involved in that level of government interest, but hearing his name meant there would be a good chance they could work things out quickly and easily, once they knew what the FBI actually wanted.

A few minutes later, he returned the phone to the cradle and stared at it for several minutes. Robert had been Brian Madson's attorney ever since the band made it big and needed legal advice. He liked working in the business sector, it being a lot cleaner than the cases he had handled long ago.

That's how he knew Jim. He knew that Godfry, a by the

book kind of guy, could be trusted at his word; a fact he had learned from working during those dark times he no longer cared to muddle through. He considered whether to call Brian back and decline the case, having heard what Godfry had to say.

Leaning back in his chair, he ran his fingers around the outside of his lips tensely. *Brian's sister is a murderer. A cold hearted bitch without remorse. She's a whore who uses men at will; completely untrustworthy and possibly sociopathic.* What's worse, the Feds weren't finished with her yet. She still had work to do for them, and they weren't going to let her go without a fight.

Scooting back up to his desk, he made the call to the number he had scratched on his notepad. Brian answered on the first ring, "Hello?" He sounded excited.

Robert began to explain to him that Tori's case was complicated, "This is going to be a bit of a struggle, Brian. I'll see what I can do, but they're going to resist our cause." He elaborated the best he could, "Also, the case has been declared classified for national security, which means going public will get us into serious trouble. We'll have to tread lightly here and do what we can."

"That's not good enough, man," Brian's voice rose with outrage, "I called you to set things straight, not make excuses why they're allowed to do this t' her!"

"I'm not saying we won't win," Frost soothed, "It just won't be fast... or easy." He would have played the expensive card as well, but he knew Brian wouldn't care about the price tag.

Michael, who anxiously listened to the conversation from Brian's end, eagerly grasped at the phone. "Hey Robert, this is Mike, former head of security for the guys. I'm also Tori's husband. Look, we want to help in whatever way we can, so what is it that you need?"

Frost paused a moment, considering the situation. "Are you guys safe there? Would they have any way of locating you?"

Michael assured him their locality was pretty secluded, and then realized Enrique had found them, presumably with help from the Feds. *Had they sent the man after us before they came to pick us up, or had it been someone else?* Back peddling slightly, he admitted, "Well, the Feds know our whereabouts for sure, if that matters."

Robert quickly agreed they were safe then, "The Feds have no intention of harming them as long as Tori does what they want her to do."

"What do you mean by that?" Michael became puzzled by his answer, "You mean they orchestrated what happened in New York?"

Robert shook his head at the device in his hand, "No, I don't think so, but they're not above manipulating the result. Let's just say, as long as she's doing what pleases them, they won't do anything to bring harm to your guys. Just stay put, but keep your eyes open. There may be other people looking for you not associated with the Feds who would be more inclined..." He trailed away, but his meaning understood.

Yeah, that's what I was afraid of. Michael hung up the phone, the concern evident on his face as Brian demanded, "Well?"

Michael only shook his head, staring at the floor while he went over the man's words slowly in his mind. *This is bad*, he thought to himself, *really bad*.

Out loud, he instructed Brian to relax. "We just lay low; you guys get a nice vacation. We can put y'all up in the motel if you want, be a little more comfortable, but we should still avoid using any of your money here, in case anyone would be able to use that to track you. And you guys need to do a better job of keeping a low profile," he gave his brother-in-law a stern look.

"Hey, I have an idea," he continued, "Let's head over to the music store where I bought Tori's guitar. We can get you some instruments. You can set them up in the garage, and use this time to maybe write some new tunes." He smiled encouragingly as he spoke. Michael had worked for the band long enough, he knew they were at their best when they could put their hearts into their music.

The pair took Tori's truck and made the purchases that afternoon. Pulling up in front of the shop to unload them, the guys were a little more calm, maybe even a little excited at the sight of their new distractions.

While they were gone picking out the equipment, the other three had cleared out the space in the garage, and all of Tori's tools and projects were pushed to the side and covered with tarps to await her return. Setting everything up was easy from there, and by midnight, the band could make plenty of racket.

As luck would have it, there were few houses close enough to be bothered as they were located more in the business district of the small town. They were free to bang away, shutting it down by midnight each day, almost happy that they had something constructive to do.

Michael watched them with a grin. *Group of big boys, they are; good kids really. Just that money changes people, as fame does.* Watching them, he thought about Tori, hoping she was ok and strong enough to endure what he knew she would have to do to get the job done.

He strongly suspected she was with Enrique, since she still had his number on a pink piece of paper in her wallet; or far as he knew. At first, the idea had bothered him, but after he had had some time to think about it, he realized it would be a good thing. *The man obviously cared about her, and that means he won't let anything happen to her if he can help it. It would almost be like she had a bodyguard.*

In the midst of his chaotic thoughts and emotions, Michael discovered one thing he knew for sure; he still loved her. And, therefore, he could not wait for her to come home so he could give her the love she really deserved.

One of the Guys

Inside groups like the Scorpions and the Dragons, there is always a pecking order, very similar to the pack mentality of wild dogs. Tori had been a part of the Dragons, but she had always been considered the lowest member, even below Henry, who had lost his position within the group after taking her without permission. The Scorpions accepted her more fully, and it became apparent she had earned a rank above many of the older members, which gave her an odd feeling.

That night, they assigned her a bunk of her own, and no one was allowed to force themselves on her after the morning Buck had beaten her with his belt before they shared her. Brett and Buck seemed to agree, she had earned her place by rights, and they would head out the next day to continue the business at hand.

Lying in her bunk alone and bored, Tori almost felt disappointed no one wanted to fuck her. She wondered how they would react if and when she did the choosing. The sex gave her a great deal of power and she felt unhappy to relinquish it so easily. As it were, lying in the dark unaccompanied, she at least had some time to think and to make her plans for the days ahead, while, at the same time, she avoided looking back as she drifted off to sleep.

Over the next week, she seemed to have forgotten about the little town in Texas and the man she had there, waiting for her return. The group had rolled out of the small camp and made their way into Colorado. Arriving in Denver, they met with a contact for The Organization, who had work for them. Taking care of several of the new jobs, her skills were verified and the respect she had gained solidified. They saw and accepted her for who and what she was, and she had nothing to hide among her peers and equals.

Within a few days, Tori began to feel a restless need rising inside of her. The only man who seemed willing to fuck her was Brett, who she entertained a few nights, but in the end, she wanted something more. When she couldn't take it any longer, she drank a large portion of a bottle of Denaka and went after Enrique, who had been keeping his distance from her since the first night they had arrived. Catching him, she insisted that he fulfill her needs.

The move quite a switch, the others watched, noting she clearly took charge of the encounter as she removed his clothes, allowing them to drop onto the ground next to a concrete picnic table in the center of their latest camp. The group had stopped at a small site, a typical location for them, and had an area laid out around it in one of the more secluded spots, comfortable in the dark open areas.

Having stripped him, she ran her hands over his bare skin. She then licked his nipples that hid beneath the hair on his chest, and dropped to her knees as he stood naked before her. Not fully aroused, he felt nervous about her actions and what it might mean within the group.

Taking him into her mouth, she excited him further and pushed him down her throat with ease. He cupped the back of her head with his hands, unable to resist her skill at pleasing men with her mouth and tongue, and small moans began escaping his tense lips.

Turning him so that he sat on the bench of the table, his back leaning against the top and legs facing out, she placed the tube of gel on the seat next to him so that he could reach it. He knew what she wanted, and he watched with hungry eyes as she undressed in front of him.

Tori still had a beautiful body in the darkness, shadows hiding the scars that marred her smooth flesh. Enrique had been nervous, but gazing at her, his desire began to push his doubts into the recesses of his mind.

By the time she slid her legs between the bench and table top to take him inside her warmth, he appeared fully prepared to do his part. Having spun the cap off the tube, he pressed on it, allowing a fair amount to coat his fingers. He then began to prepare her for the position she tried to pretend she hated. His fingers worked skillfully, and she kissed him, purring, "You know how I like it, baby." She smiled, and he played along with her without hesitation.

Enrique grinned wickedly as she lifted herself enough for him to take the new position, allowing gravity to bring her body down slowly on top of him. The stretching uncomfortable at first, they took it slow for a few minutes, so she could relax and accept him fully. His hands moved over her body, and he nuzzled her face with his nose, reassured that he loved and wanted his nasty bitch. More than pleased to be with her, he whispered, "I missed you, baby girl," into her hair.

Tori drove him to the edge, and then paused, holding still until she could move again. Smiling at him, she caressed the nape of his neck, her fingers running through his ebony waves. She knew he saw through her, and she had nothing to hide when she fucked him, their darkness equally matched.

She could always blame it on the liquor, but deep down she knew she liked what they did in the night.

Soon, her legs grew tired and he pushed her to slide off of him, laying her across the table on her belly so that her legs hung down to the ground. Lying over her back as he reclaimed his point of entry, he rubbed the length of her back and side. Taking his time for a few moments, he began to move in quick deep strokes until he had finished himself, leaving her still on edge.

He had stopped pulsing, and slid himself out, stepping back to clean his softening flesh and enjoy the show. Tori suddenly felt ill at ease, never having actually been in charge on the nights like this. Surveying the group as they waited, she became reassured of the power she held over them.

Wanting to express her desires, she pushed herself up, looking for someone to come forward and volunteer. Seeing that none would be that bold, she swung her gaze over them and realized she did not care who would be next. She just needed someone, this being her chance to take the upper hand.

Catching Buck's gaze, she stared at him insistently, curling up onto the table in a naked pose; willing him to come and pick up where Enrique had left off. Slowly, he approached the table to test the waters. Reaching out to him as he neared her, she used her charms to draw him in, and began to undress him with a grasping motion, freeing his belt from the lower portion of his anatomy.

Running the fingers of his left hand through her hair, his right hand moved up, sliding his palm roughly along her curves. Closing her eyes and relaxing into the coarseness of his grasp, she found the outlet for her need that Enrique had neglected to fully quench. The growing eagerness of his hands made them rough as he massaged her breasts and toyed with the nipples, but she cooed softly to him, urging him to continue.

Turning her to face the table once more, he pushed her down as he worked himself out of his trousers and unceremoniously inserted himself into his preferred location. He made no effort to conceal his pleasure at being permitted to fuck her, even if he was not allowed to beat her beforehand.

When he finished, the rest came forward easily, confident in her intent. Like so many times before, none were turned away. No marks were left on her and she had been fully satiated by the time she passed out in the darkness.

The next morning, Tori lay on the ground under the table, wrapped in a sleeping bag. A fire had been built and they provided her with a pot of heated water to clean herself. The mood almost jovial, the group seemed pleased she had decided to become one of the guys, but retain her prior role as well. As she surveyed the group, she knew her deeds would indeed give her power, but it held little consolation to her at the moment.

Tori poured over the guilt of her actions as she used the warm liquid to wash away the evidence of her transgressions. Her head ached from the liquor, and she thought about her purpose there in the first place; unable to push the thoughts aside any longer.

Her husband and brother were down in Texas, hiding from the men she hung out with, *like I'm on vacation or something*. God knows they were probably worried about her, at least she knew Michael would be. These thoughts tore at her heart, and she knew she would never tell him how she had cheated on him.

Not in the motel with Enrique. That had been a necessary part of the plan. Not the times Brett had tossed her to them like a dog is given a bone. She could absolve herself from those moments, having no other option.

However, what happened last night, she had allowed, and she did it for her own satisfaction. She could tell herself otherwise, but deep down she knew the truth. She hung her head as she realized she had enjoyed what they had done to her. *You're a drunken whore, and nothing more*, she berated herself coldly. *And Michael is more than you deserve.*

Never before had she allowed herself to take responsibility in that manner. She had never been so ashamed of herself in her life, and she knew she needed to get on with the task at hand, before she became too lost in the role she played to ever find her way home.

Age of Innocence

Awakening alone in their queen-sized bed on the first of July, Michael's heart felt heavy in his chest. Lying on his side so he could peer out the window on the front side of the house, he had a clear view of her favorite tree. He watched the shadows begin to fade as the sun peeked over the horizon. Spinning his ring on his left hand with his thumb, he remembered watching her as she stretched beneath the limbs, ages ago, with a small smile on his lips.

Rising, he dressed for a quick run and a few sets to start the day. He had been struggling to keep their routine the best he could in her absence, and lying in bed pining over her was not an option. Taking a quick round of the neighborhood, he returned to the tree to do squats and pushups before turning to rest against the rough bark.

Tori had only been gone a few weeks, but for Michael it had seemed an eternity. His four house guests had reluctantly accepted the rules he had finally seen fit to give them, and were keeping to themselves for the most part, content to work on their music in the tiny shop or lounge around watching television in the small living room during the day.

Michael had quickly become bored with babysitting the men. He had also grown tired of feeling at the mercy of his thoughts and fears. Leaning against the tall mesquite to recoup after his workout, he considered his options. *There's gotta be something around here that I can do; some task that'll keep me busy and still make a difference down the line.*

Watching the light of early morning grow brighter, he realized he needed to put his efforts into building towards their future. Since the shop was otherwise engaged, he needed something else to put his hands on, and after a few dazed moments of staring at their quaint domain, he knew the thing that would do the trick.

Michael had never really been into school, preferring the carpentry and shop classes that had paid off so richly as he and Tori had remodeled their home. It had been that success that sparked his interest in the old Victorian style house that Marge maintained alone. Standing from his reclined position, he made his way back inside to shower and change before he rode over to make his intentions known.

His mind still deep in thought as he dressed, Michael stood in the bedroom that the couple shared, staring into his wallet at the white piece of paper hidden there. *Keep this safe for me*, her note read. *She's coming back.* Peering at the scrap, he ran his finger across her smooth print, allowing it to give him strength to face the day. *She has to be coming back.*

Back outside, Michael climbed onto his bike and rode the few blocks over, past the café, to visit the older woman. The morning quiet in the sleepy town, the temperature remained low, but would climb with the sun as it moved high enough to bring on the heat of a mid-summer afternoon. Taking the short flight of stairs of the porch in twos, his heart began to pound with excitement.

Having a look around, he had already begun to survey the

amount of work that would be needed to make the house their home. Michael rapped lightly on the screen door as he thought about the older woman who resembled his own mother to a degree, and how the events of their lives had entwined and unfolded.

The couple had visited with Marge on the night of their wedding reception. Thinking back, he recalled how she informed them of her late husband's fondness for his wife. George had sold the shop to them solely due to her bold moves and refusal to allow him to turn her away. Perched on his couch, she had stared at him with crystal blue orbs of hope, drawing him in and bending him to her will. *Tori has that effect on people and can often get her way with just a look.*

Afterwards, on their way to New York, Michael had made up his mind that the couple should someday have the house. They would pour their love into it as they had done for the shop and small dwelling behind it, bringing life back to the old and neglected structure. *Yeah, this's a good plan, I'm sure of it,* he grinned eagerly.

Snapping his attention back to the elderly woman who stood staring at him through the wire screen, Michael gave her a wide smile and a jovial greeting, "Good morning!"

She eyed him suspiciously, "Well, this's a surprise. You here alone?"

Michael only nodded in an exaggerated fashion and moved away from the entrance so she could join him on the porch.

Seeing he intended to speak to her, Marge pushed the door with a labored shove and moved out to join him on the veranda, then took a seat on the swing directly. First seeing to it that she rested comfortably, Michael then sat, back leaned against the corner post of the railing facing her, right foot dropped onto the next step in a relaxed position.

He opened the conversation in a friendly manner, making small talk, "So, how've you been doing?" He held his smile firm, noting she had not returned his warm greeting.

A shrewd woman, she spat in a clipped tone, "Now, I know you've got somethin' up yur sleeve, no other reason fur you t' be here," glaring at him while she waited.

Michael briefly paused, wiping at his lips with his nervous fingers, "Indeed I do. I want your house," his brown eyes flashed with excitement.

The older woman stared at him slack jawed, not accustomed to the forwardness of the stranger who was obviously not from around the small town and its simple way of life. She knew Tori had used an accent similar to a local to convince her husband to sell her the garage, but the pair were outsiders. It had later been a point of contention between the older couple when it became obvious that she had been conniving and deceitful to gain the old man's trust and approval.

Georgie thought it was funny, how she tricked 'im and made 'im look foolish. Her husband felt it had been a bold move on the part of the young woman, an act that showed her earnestness and true desire to follow her dream. He had liked that about the girl, and admired her deeply for her intrepidity and hardworking nature.

Glaring at Michael, Marge drew a deep breath, allowing her eyes to take in the dilapidated state of the wood that could be seen from her vantage point. Absently, she asked, "You know this house's called a Victorian... Th' Age o' Innocence."

Giving her a small smile, he encouraged her to go on, "So it is. I take it that means a great deal to you."

Shrugging slightly, she explained, "This house is a reflection o' simpler times, when women were meek, an' they was submissive." Her words held a sharp edge, and she glared at the younger man, knowing his wife to be neither of those things. "I never liked that girl, not frum the moment I laid eyes on 'er. She's a devious wench, an' there ain't no way o' her livin' in my home. Makes me sick t' m' stomach, even t' consider it." She hardened her heart to the idea of the couple ever owning her beloved palace as long as she lived to prevent it.

Michael sat on the step, nodding to the matriarch's assessment of his bride. When she had finished her scathing torrent, he smiled. "Yeah, I get how you could see her that way. But I believe that you're truly a good soul, and so I'm about to share something with you that no one else in this tiny town knows."

Marge's grey eyes bore into him, "Unlikely you'll change m' mind, but by all means, have yur say." She wafted a shaky, crinkled hand at him as she spoke.

Nodding, he leaned forward slightly as he explained, "My wife needs this house. I completely agree with your assessment, your description of the way women were meant to be, and I'll be the first to admit, she's never been like other women. Never been... respectable."

He rocked his jaw side to side as he considered his words carefully, "But Tori's hand was stacked against her when she was a little girl, and a man who wanted her for a dark purpose stepped in and changed her destiny."

Marge blinked at him, unreadable at the moment.

Michael used his hands to illustrate his story and support his cause as he pushed on. "He murdered her parents and covered his tracks, taking her before she was even old enough to go to school. Took her away from everyone and everything she knew."

"They took south, to Brazil, and raised her in a primitive camp, teaching her the things she would need to be and do the things they wanted her to do. And when she was ready, they inducted her into the group, taking her brutally against her will… repeatedly beating her and forcing themselves on her, until it was clear she had no choice but to accept the fate they had in store for her. You said she should be submissive, and I attest to you that she was, or they'd've killed her."

The things he described gave Marge a chill, and she became visibly shaken by his gruesome tale. She had lived a sheltered life, not having known such brutality truly existed in the world from her simple and protected point of view. Seeing her shifting features, Michael adjusted his tone.

He explained calmly how the girl had gone along with the whims of the coldhearted swine, "And finally, when she couldn't stand anymore, she raised her hand against them to gain her freedom. She left their bodies soaked in blood, and even tried to end her own life out of guilt and shame."

"But she was saved. And now she struggles to find a new life; a new way to live, if you will." Drawing close to the end, he indicated the wide expanse of the world with a wave of his hand. "She's out there right now, somewhere. She's workin' to keep others from finding this place, to preserve the peace she found in our little town, in hopes that she might someday return to it forever."

"She needs this house," he stated again. "She needs the chance to make a choice, to live the life she wants, not the life she is forced to endure. You have all given her so much, even more than you can possibly imagine, taking her in as you have. Her first meal with a family, the one we shared after George's funeral. It meant so much to her."

Marge stiffened, recalling how angry she had been that Trish had brought the whore into her home to dine with her beloved kin on such an occasion. Staring at him with pursed lips, she said nothing, keeping the memory to herself in her forced silence.

"We want to restore it," he stated calmly. "That's what

she does. She takes things, and she fixes them. The small apartment and the garage; we made them new again. It's what she does with the motorcycles that she rebuilds, taking the broken and mending it. It's what this house can help her do for herself. It can help her find her inner innocence." Michael used the woman's own words against her. *Tori isn't the only one who can be persuasive.*

He inhaled deeply, seeing the softening of the older woman's jaw as she listened. Shaking his head slightly, he asked, "Would you deny someone you loved the chance to get better? Time to recover from an illness?" He saw the look of pain that shot across her creased features, knowing she thought of her late husband.

"Tori has the chance to heal, to move beyond that horrific past. Would you give her that? This woman I love so much, I would risk everything we have? You must know that telling you this is a risk, but it's one I had to take." He pushed on, his brown eye's pleading as he had watched Tori's do long ago. Staring at the elderly woman, he could see she wasn't ready to give in.

Rising from the step, he knew he had time to let her stew on the matter. "I don't expect an answer at this exact moment. I'll come back to help you with the yard work, and whatever else you might need a hand with in a few days." He presented her with his best smile as he turned to go.

Giving him a sour scowl, "I don't need yur help," she snapped at him, "I got family that'll do that fur me. I don't need nothin' frum you."

With a small wave, Michael left her to think about what he had said. A man of his word, he would return in a few days, look after her as he had promised, and hopefully in time acquire that place of serenity his love so desperately needs.

Fallen Angel

Tori felt beaten, realizing she could not control her physical urges. Once the sun set, she could only think about two things: liquor and sex, and not necessarily in that order. Her purpose with the group quickly become jumbled, as she took the men at will, fully understanding she held a great power over them, and they over her.

She had always known she could use her body to get her way at times, but now it came too easy. They watched her, lust in their eyes, and she ate it up like a kid with a bucket full of Halloween candy. *This is so different than the Dragons. Jesus Christ, how do I stop it?*

Enrique would have liked to say he felt disappointed, but deep down, he seemed more pleased with the outcome than she did. She could see a side of him that had been hidden in LA, and it did little to boost her trust in him, as she realized it did not bother this man to share her, and she found herself avoiding him whenever she could.

Brett, however, wasn't happy, growing sullen as he realized she did not truly belong to him by choice. To make matters worse, the group often deferred to her judgment

106

rather than his. He had never been heavy handed with the Scorpions, the leader more or less by appointment. No one had ever challenged him for the lead. That foundation had become unstable, and he did not like the way it felt, knowing she could topple him at will.

Tori could tell Brett felt threatened, and made it a point to pull him aside to a private corner in the early darkness of their latest makeshift camp. She intended to allow her body to do the talking, confident that she could ease his mind with a little physical persuasion.

Kissing him, she ran her hands easily over his tense limbs. Catching her fingers, he chided, "I really don' wanna be with you." She only smiled, and pulled away, opening and spreading their sleeping bags on top of one another. She bent over so that her rear end waved around extensively in the process. Kicking off her boots, she stood them upright, next to the pallet, and looked up at him with big blue eyes.

Brett stared down at her, willing himself to walk away. She had given up on the makeup almost as soon as they left Ohio, and he could see the scar that covered her left eye easily in the dim light. Always beautiful to him, he swallowed hard as he became conscious that his feet were planted unmovably on the spot.

Rising to her feet in front of him, she ran the fronts of her fingers firmly along his legs to his waist. Pausing there, she slid them around behind for a moment, a weak embrace that pushed her breasts lightly against his chest as she breathed into the soft curve of his neck.

He could feel the stiffness of her nipples teasing him through their shirts, and he reluctantly realized his body had responded to her, sensing his pants begin to tighten. Grasping the hem of his tee, she lifted it up and he raised his arms, allowing her to pull it off and drape it over the tops of her boots.

Struggling to hold himself together, he took a step back, but she only used the opportunity to unhook his belt buckle and slide it off as well. Closing the distance between them, she nuzzled his ear, blowing warm air against it, almost purring. She was taller than him, a fact that had always excited him a little, and as her fingers danced across his bare skin, he could feel his resolve slipping away.

Pulling at his jeans, she freed the button and unzipped the front, her fingers pushing down to wrap themselves around his expanding flesh. She panted, her excitement evident. She toyed with him, causing a small amount of sticky liquid to ooze from his stiff shaft, and he lost all hope of resisting her.

His hands raked across her waist roughly, tugging at her shirt and hoisted it over her head. Unclasping her bra, he freed her mounds of womanhood, running his digits across them, his hunger growing.

Tori released him long enough to remove her own pants, lying on the ground to kick her way out of them. Tossing them aside, she rolled up onto her knees, clutching the sides of his and pulling them down so that he could feel the cool night air on his nakedness, her mouth tantalizing his tender skin.

Brett had always felt displeased at the size of his equipment, like he was not worthy somehow, or God had played a sick joke on him when creating him. Tori always made him feel like it didn't matter, just as she did that night.

She took what he had to offer, never making him feel like it wasn't enough. He closed his eyes as she worked him, his hands resting on the top of her head. *Damn it*, he cursed himself. *You know this ain't real for her, why you let 'er do this t' you?*

Tori slid him out of her mouth, pulling him down onto the mat beside her. She persuaded him to lie flat, and he followed her command, powerless to deny her. Her hands were hot as they moved over him in the cool air, and she took her time to caress and kiss his taught muscles, tugging his boots and jeans off to get them out of the way.

Brett enjoyed the breeze that encircled his skin, a sharp contrast to her scorching flesh that teased him. She had grown sufficiently moist during her petting, and slid her smooth legs over so that she could straddle him and take him inside her warm folds.

Leaning over him, she moved in slow motion, waiting for his desire to be ignited and persuade him to take the lead. She did not have to wait long before he grasped the roundness of her rear end and lifted his hips to push himself inside her in short quick thrusts. She could feel him hitting that special spot within her as she held herself up in a position between lying and sitting and her eyes rolled uncontrollably as her body trembled.

She clawed at his shoulders as her limbs shook, the weakened tickle in her hands confirming he had finished her with ease. There had been few men to ever do this for her. She realized this as she stared down into his green eyes, unable to move, feeling the heaviness after being slaked.

Brett had finished himself almost as soon as her tremors began, and lay stroking the length of her back, meeting her stare without remorse. *My fallen angel*, he thought to himself as he held her, *the only woman I've ever cared to own.*

Soon, the cool air became too much, and the pair worked their way between the sleeping bags, snuggling against one another for warmth. Tori lay in the crook of his arm, stroking the few hairs that dotted his broad chest with her left hand.

An older man, Brett would be near fifty best she could determine. He had been a cohort of Red and Eddie, and she wondered exactly when, how and why they had met. Trying to be casual about the question, she put it to him in a gentle whisper, "So, you were an old friend of the guys?"

Reaching up with his right hand, he caught her wandering fingers and laced them with his own. Holding her hand against his chest, he deliberated his words, suspecting gleaning the information to be the real reason she had lain with him so readily. "Men like Eddie an' Red Farrell don' have frien's." Rubbing his thumb along the crease of her hand, he waited.

Tori lay still for a moment, listening to the thump of his heart inside his chest. She found the sound comforting, like the nights she had lain next to Henry in the darkness of Brazil. Before any man had touched her; before she knew what the world was like.

Allowing him to keep her hand, she pushed herself up onto her right elbow so she could stare into his face. "You don't trust me, do you?" Her tone flat, she assumed she was correct in her assessment.

Meeting her gaze, Brett continued to take his time in responding. "I knew th' men that raised you. I can't say that I have much faith in what you say an' do." Seeing the pain flicker across her face before she squashed it, he clarified, "It ain't yur fault, ya know. They did it t' you. Made you cold... calculated. It served their purpose."

Staring at his lips, "And what exactly was their purpose?" She asked the question, but she already knew the answer. She wanted to hear what he would say. *I want to know how much he knows.*

"I know who you are, baby girl." His response surprised her, as that was not where she thought her words would lead. "They formed their plan almos' as soon as we hired on with Th' Organization. Twenty-one, twenty-two years ago now. It took almos' a year for him to choose you. We rode together back then, but things were busy an' we needed more guys."

"I volunteered to head up a new group, put together th' crew that rides with me now, what's left of 'em. That way

110

the Dragons could hold up in Brazil while they trained you, only comin' north when th' seasons were right." He toyed with her hair that hung over his hand behind her, caressing the warm flesh of her bare back.

"Who am I then, if I might be so bold?" She still didn't even know her own name, so if he chose to lie, it wouldn't matter. He didn't, and the utterance brought a flood of new memories streaming into her crowded brain.

"Yur name was Nikki. Nichole Peters. Brian Peters changed his name to Madson when he became famous. He… is yur brother." He spoke the words quietly, revealing how he had known which tree to shake to locate her. "Fortunately, I knew Eddie sent Michael Anderson, Henry's brother, to watch him. Smart man Eddie was. Always planned ahead. He knew he might have to use Brian someday, in case you needed a li'l encouragement somewhere down the line. Tha's why he didn' take you 'til it was jus' you, and yur parents."

"And how did he do that?" she asked quietly, not sure she really wanted to hear any more. *My God, he knew everything, even before I told him what he wanted to know,* she recalled the day she arrived in Ohio, and the night he had interrogated her.

"You don' remember?" queried, surprised she had forgotten. "Think hard, baby girl. Tell me what you know."

Frowning, Tori pulled her hand away, turning her back on him in the darkness. Clutching at the thick cloth in front of her chest, she suddenly wished she had gotten dressed; being naked next to him had grown uncomfortable.

Brett let her lie for a moment in her half curled position, giving her time to relax. Eventually, he spooned up behind her, laying his arm across her body in a protective manner, his face lying against the hair that covered her ear. Gripping her tightly, he breathed warm air across the side of her face and waited.

Bit by Bit

"I've been getting memories back for a while. Bit by bit. Should have known I would eventually have them all. Were you there? The day they took me?" She trembled beneath the covers and he tightened his arm around her.

"No. I knew th' plan, but I had work t' do, gatherin' guys t' form th' Scorpions." He nuzzled her ear as he spoke, enjoying the scent of her.

"I remember my brother. I remember us playing together, or rather me chasing after him. He was always telling me to go away. I hated that." She sighed deeply at the memory, Brian never wanting her around, even when they were kids. She scowled, almost certain his name wasn't Brian, either. *At least, that's not what I called him.*

"That day, the day it all happened, we took him to some place with a green barn. Our grandparent's place I think. I remember I wanted to stay there, but he wouldn't let me. So we left. Afterwards, I was crying. I never liked not getting my way, and I was trying to make my parents feel bad about not leaving me at the farm." She paused, the thought of them coming to her, the pictures she had seen in Brian's study awakening a clear image of them in her mind.

"We stopped at a diner to eat. Mommy and daddy were trying to console me." She spoke sharply, almost angry at the recollection and the pain its return had brought her. "They promised me a treat. But I wanted more. Our food had arrived, and some guys came in… guys in leather and boots. One of them touched me on top of the head as they passed behind my chair. I remember looking up at him. It was Red…" her voice trailed away, lost in the surging remembrances.

Not having any fear of the large man above her, the young girl had looked up at him and smiled. As soon as the two men were seated, her mother had insisted they had to leave, immediately. She never specified why, and Nikki's father had been irritated, but willing to do as she requested.

Realizing they were leaving before she would get her bribe, Nikki grew angry again, loudly throwing a tantrum when they placed her into the back seat of their car. Pulling her favorite bear out of her bag, her mother twisted around from the front as her father drove, trying to quiet her and stop the flow of shrill shrieks.

Talking to her daughter soothingly, something out the back glass had frozen her face in fear, and Tori had ever since been haunted by the scream that escaped her mother's lips the instant before the car was struck and spun off the road. That's what she had dreamt so many times over the years. Her mother's expression of horror, the scream, and the image of the fire after she had been pulled from the wreckage and placed on the motorcycle as shots rang out.

Nikki sat, straddling a bike and facing the man who carried her. She had dropped her bear, and leaned over to peer under his arm to find it, lying on the ground a short distance from the burning shell of their car. Clinging to the stranger, she had cried loudly, the wind of the bike scaring her as her long hair whipped around her shivering body.

She had no idea how far they had ridden. She only knew they stopped in a gas station and she was taken into the bathroom by one of the men. She later realized that it had been Eddie Farrell, who stripped her and gave her a new set of clothes to put on. Nikki had been upset at being made to remove her beloved dress, and wanted no part of the pants and long sleeved shirt that were placed before her.

Eddie laughed loudly as he grabbed her arms and forced the shirt over her head. Getting the pants onto her in a similar manner, he finished with a loud grunt, "Now, your new name is Tori. Tori Farrell. If anyone asks, that's all *you* are allowed to say." He poked her in the chest as he spoke to accentuate the word *you*, and must have thought she would be afraid of him, but on the contrary, she was pissed.

"My name is Nikki. Nikki Peters. Nichole Peters." She had no fear of calling him wrong to his face, and he slapped her, the sting causing her eyes to burn. Tears running down her face, the argument continued for some time, his blows growing more incessant as he struck her on the arms and chest, and then legs, trying to drive his point home.

Eventually, another man pushed his way into the tiny room to inform the group's leader that their display had become public knowledge; the attendant could hear their confrontation going on from outside. His blood boiling red across his face, Eddie had pointed to the girl, "You better fix this, or we'll have to dump her."

Something about the way this man had looked at her as Eddie went out to take care of the nosey clerk moved the little girl. His eyes were a deep chocolate, his hair a mix of sandy blonde and deep brown with glistening curls.

He knelt down on the bathroom floor in front of her, his words calm in his thick gruff voice, "Listen now, baby girl. You gotta use yur new name. If you don', things're gonna end badly fur you. I'm gonna take care o' you if ya let me, but you can't make Eddie mad like that. He'll take you away from me if you do."

Silently studying the gentle giant for a moment, the tears still dripped from her quivering chin. Standing, he reached over and grasped a handful of brown paper towels from the metal box on the wall. Wetting them in the sink, he washed her tiny cheeks. Staring at her crystal blue eyes, he soothed, "See, now that's a good girl. I'm Henry. Henry Morgan." He offered his hand to her and she shook it fearlessly.

A moment later, Eddie came back to the door, informing his group mate it was time to go. "Are we leavin' her body here or is she comin' with us?"

Hearing his tone, Tori reached to grasp Henry's fingers as he replied, "Naw, man, she's good. Jus' needed a bit o' persuadin'." He smiled down at her upturned face and led her out to his bike, where she sat in front of him, facing him so that she could cling to his chest with his jacket wrapped around her as she rode.

Tori awoke the next morning in the early light of dawn, Brett still gripping her tightly, as he had held her while she cried herself to sleep. She felt so broken lying next to him, this man who had known the truth about her all these years, and done nothing about it. She felt angry at him, but in the end, what choice did he have?

Pushing back against him, she began to stretch, and he released his hold on her, allowing her to roll onto her back and face him. She had shared her memories with him, all that she had from the day her parents had died. She felt connected to him, tied in the sharing and the pain it had released, calming her somehow. Staring into his eyes, she waited patiently for him to decide his next move. When he stirred to kiss her, she parted her lips, equaling his fervor.

Moving above her, Brett separated her legs and made his way between them, taking her easily in the morning chill. The sleeping bag spread over them, their bodies meshed and collided while neither uttered a sound. Tori stared into his green eyes as he moved above her, her hands taking in the breadth of his strong shoulders and muscular chest. Gripping his warm red curls, she pulled his mouth to hers and kissed him eagerly, holding him until he had been satisfied, and they were ready to begin a new day.

Stubborn Women

Michael could tell something was wrong with her. He had been coming over for a couple of hours every other day or so for over a week. So far, he had cleaned up the yard, mowed the grass, and made sure all of the trees and shrubs had water. There had also been a large rosebush in the back that had long since been dead, and it took him the better part of a day to dig it up and remove it.

The first day he had arrived, Marge had given him another list of reasons she did not need his help. Ignoring her, he had settled on the outside chores, focusing on them until she trusted him enough to let him inside.

Going back into the house, she had pretended he wasn't there, or tried to, cowering and peeking at him through windows until he had had enough of the work and the July heat, and headed home.

The second day, she had felt a little bolder, taking up a seat on the back steps to watch as he dealt with the weeds and grass out back. When he pulled off his shirt to combat the rising temperature, she had to admit he was a good looking man. She was after all old, not dead. Taking her time, she made her way into the kitchen to fetch him a glass of ice water, and gave him a small smile when he thanked her for it.

Tilting the container to drink it, his muscles rippled beneath the flesh on his chest, and she caught a glimpse of the small motorcycle hiding in the hairs there. Underneath it, she could scarcely make out the letters, T-O-R-I.

Noting her staring at the spot, Michael ran his hand across it anxiously, thinking about his wife and the day they had gotten their matching marks. Taking the empty glass from him, Marge moved slowly as she made her way back up the steps and into the house without further comment.

A week later, he warmed a chair at her small kitchen table, staring at her as she slowly washed the dishes, wondering how to approach the subject. Rising, he picked up the cup-towel and began to dry the plates as she placed them in the drainer. Together they finished the small task, and he hung the rag over the edge of the cabinet as he commented, "So, what did the doctor say?"

Turning, she gave him a surprised look. "What doctor?" she demanded incredulously.

"The one you need to see," he stated matter-of-factly, looking down his nose at her.

"Oh, is that how it is. You cut my grass, you think you can tell me what t' do now?" she stared at him straight on, her blue eyes flashing.

"Someone needs to," he remained steadfast, "You're not well. I can see it. Does Trish know?" Seeing the angry look that fluttered across her wrinkled features, he surmised the answer to be no.

The older woman turned and shuffled her way into the living room, to sit on the ancient sofa and rest.

Following her, Michael recalled how she had looked the day he and Tori had first arrived at the house. *It's a real*

118

shame how quickly she's gone downhill. Helping her to find her seat on the cushion, he then knelt down in front of her, gazing intently at her face and waiting for her to give him a straight answer.

"Don' no body have time for an ol' woman like me," she huffed at him. "Now, you go on, do whatever it is yur here fur, an' jus' let me have a rest." Her southern drawl sounded tired, and she breathed heavily, even after she had finished speaking.

Leaving her, he made himself busy cleaning up the room and assessing the staircase. Determining it would need some repairs, he inquired if she had a tape measure.

"All Georgie's tools are out in th' shed, in th' back," she wheezed as she waved her hand in that general direction.

Leaving her for the few minutes it would take to retrieve a few items, Michael slipped out to the small shack and gathered up a handful of equipment. Back inside, he measured the slats that would need to be replaced, as well as the length of the case for a new railing. Jotting down the information, he planned to head to the hardware store before returning home.

Noticing how she watched him, he only shook his head. He had known his share of stubborn women. *Hell, I married one*. He knew what to do about it, though. *Nothing. Just do what you gotta do, and she'll come around.*

Once all the measurements had been taken, he made his way back over to his elderly neighbor to assess her condition. She appeared more normal, the color returned to her pudgy lips. She managed a smile, inquiring if she passed inspection.

Michael grinned, "For now, yes. You need any help getting upstairs?"

She gave him a shake of her short white waves, "No, son, I'll make it jus' fine. You go on, get home wit ya. I'll see ya in th' mornin'."

119

He noted she assumed he would return the next day. And of course, he would. She had become more than just a distraction. She genuinely needed him there, even if she couldn't admit it. *Stubborn women*, he muttered to himself has he exited through the screen door, careful not to let it slam behind him.

Things in Motion

Tori found herself thinking about Sir Isaac Newton and his first law, the law of inertia. *Things in motion stay in motion, unless acted upon by an unbalanced force.* She had put her plan in motion; her desire to take out the Scorpions and bring peace to her life once and for all.

Her hidden needs had been an unbalanced force, but she had learned to control them and used them to her advantage. In the end, her plan moved forward, almost better than she could have hoped. The group completely trusted her, Brett ever watchful of their actions towards her. She could tell he had feelings for her. *I own him in fact*, the thought made her smile, and between him and Enrique, she knew she was well guarded.

During the time since her arrival in the group, she had come into several valuable pieces of information. The first one being, this group was nowhere near the caliber of her former crew. If it had not been for their numbers, she would have already killed them in their sleep and been done with them.

However, sleeping close quarters as they did, she could

not risk such a brash move. She knew she would get her chance as they could not always be together, every minute of every day.

The Dragons had been made entirely of military men. Some had been Special Forces, a few Marines, and Marcus and Paul had been SEALS. All of them were well trained, and they had imparted their wisdom to her as fully as they had been able.

The Scorpions, on the other hand, held only three ex-military. Brett, Buck and Enrique were all former SF. The rest of the guys, at least nine of them, were true street thugs. Not that they couldn't handle whatever work The Organization handed to them. They were good at following orders, and with Brett and Buck to do their planning, they worked as a functional unit that could be considered acceptable, but no more than that. That left the one, Geek they called him, who she still did not have a clear bead on; but she worked on that when she could.

Looking at them as she ate her dinner, Tori began to think about this fact, as well as the other information she had discovered. She had been with the group for four weeks, and had pretty much secluded herself, only fucking them when she wanted something from them, as this made them much more pliable to her desires. Staring at the one she had determined to have taken Enrique's place, she decided they were in need of some time together as there were a few things she needed to know.

A quiet, nerdy sort, she had noticed that he had declined taking his turns at her the few times they had been permitted before she earned her rank. Even after, he avoided her, a bit shy of the girl who had shown up and proceeded to shake everything up in their tightknit group.

Moving over next to him, she cooed softly to him, plying him with questions and giving him her best wide-eyed expressions. She had seen him with his little laptop, and come to realize he knew things about computers and other electronic devices. She wanted him to teach her what he knew, to enlighten her about these things, and would be willing to use her womanly charms to convince him to share.

Geek's reaction startled her. He had never tasted her before when she had been forced, not that kind of man she presumed. Now that she made advances, he didn't trust her and kept his distance again. This confused her to an extent, and for the first time she considered the possibility that he might be gay.

Hinting at her suspicion, he chuckled at her. Without comment, he had walked away, leaving her to wonder about the odd kid who did not quite mesh with the rough crowd around them.

Watching as the group spread out for the night, Tori thought about what she knew, and decided she would have to find a way to make him trust her. Keeping her clothes on and curling up in her bag, she feigned exhaustion, and pretended to be in deep sleep right away. Waiting patiently, the rest of the crew followed suit and she moved around in the moonlight to set up her plan after they had fallen asleep.

Pulling out a couple of tools, she went over to Geek's bike and went to work. Loosening a few parts, she made the adjustment. *Something small it would take a bit to kick in. Something I can repair easily later, once we've set out tomorrow. Done.* She grinned slyly as she replaced the tools in their bag and made her way back to her pack.

The next morning, the group rolled out, heading into a small town and locating the diner. Falling about the place, they ate a hearty meal while a few of the guys harassed the waitress. Tori watched coolly, confidence dripping from her as she surveyed them and gave Brett a small smile.

He had become more comfortable with her lately, safe in

his role as leader. He still wished he could call her his alone, but he knew she was fucking Enrique regularly, as she made no attempt to hide the fact. Seeing her tiny grin made his heart flutter slightly. *At least she seems happy to be a part of us, even if I have to share.*

He recalled how he had offered his entire life's savings to buy her from Eddie, even going so far as to offer to wait for delivery until she had completed her special task and the Dragons were done with her. *How did she do this to me, and make it look so easy?*

He chuckled as he recalled that Enrique suspected her of witchcraft, and pondered what kind of test they could perform to find out if it were true. *I never used the L-word in my life… I'm sure as hell not gonna start,* although he could not help but suspect it to be true.

Finishing their meal, they made their way outside to fill their tanks and prepare for a long day's ride as they had a job in Vegas and would be hard put to get there if they delayed any longer. Preparing to climb on behind Brett, Tori worked him, boosting his confidence in her commitment to him and the Scorpions further. However, a small commotion had begun, and it became apparent there was a problem: Geek's bike wouldn't start.

Making their way over, Brett inspected the engine in a cursory manner, swearing loudly at the machine. Apparently a common occurrence for it to give them problems, having the delay had been nothing out of the ordinary. Except on this particular day, they had no time for it.

Kneeling down next to her companion, Tori offered in a sweet voice, "I could stay behind with him. Make the repairs and the two of us catch up to you."

Brett eyed her for a moment, not sure he trusted her that completely yet. Standing slowly, he swung his gaze around the group. Anyone else staying behind would mean losing two of their rides for the time being. That, or two of the men having to double up.

Growling, he kicked a small rock across the blacktop. Looking back at her squarely, he could see she waited patiently beside him. *Waiting for me to choose.* Staring into her clear blue eyes, he knew he would to have to trust her some time. *Damn it.*

"Alright, grab th' tool bag and fix it up. Enrique, give 'er yur cell." He paused long enough to ensure she held the tiny device. Pointing at it, he continued, "My number is saved inside. Call when ya hit the road so we know you're on yur way. And don't forget to charge it."

"I won't," she tucked the small cord into Geek's saddlebag.

Surprised by the look in Brett's eyes as he watched her, *is he worried about me, or about losing me?* She knew there was a difference. Taking the time to give him a long, sensual kiss, she cemented his faith that he had made the right choice. *Later, love*, she mentally taunted him. Overjoyed by her apparent success, she nuzzled his cheek for affect.

Swinging onto their bikes, the rowdiest members of the group made their exit, leaving Tori and her new friend standing next to his gimped motorcycle. He looked at her dubiously, a bit surprised she would know how to fix it.

"Here," she commanded when they were gone, "Let's push it over out of the way."

Lining the wheels up along the sidewalk that ran down the side of the café, they would have some protection from the wind and sun as the day wore on. Kneeling down next to the machine, she began to make her inspection, using some of the tools to remove a few bolts and poke around.

Geek knelt down next to her, his eyes wide as he watched her nimble fingers. "You actually know about bikes?" he truly felt in awe of her at that moment.

"Of course. I lived with the Dragons my whole life." She gave him a small smile, as if he should have known that fact.

Shaking his head, he countered lightly, "Naw, I don't know any Dragons. All I know are these guys... and the Spiders."

The mention of the third group startled her, but she did not want to let on it had been a surprise. She knew about them, but had never met any of the other teams that worked for The Organization.

He remained silent for a while, watching her work. Finally, his curiosity got the better of him and he began to ply her with questions. "You're not like the other girls. The ones the group takes, dumpin' their bodies when they're done with them." He made the observation slowly, then pushed on with a furrowed brow, "Why do you stay with them?"

Without meeting his gaze, she bantered evenly, "Why do *you* stay with them?"

Geek looked struck, realizing that she knew his situation. "I can't leave." He faltered a bit, unhappy at the admission, and she only nodded in reply.

"I thought it would be cool, ya know? Join up with a biker gang, ride aroun' bein' tough. They seemed really interested in havin' me, but after I helped them get that other guy back," he shrugged, "They lost interest. I can't leave though; not allowed." His shoulders drooped as he stared inside the tool bag.

"Yep," she replied in a calm voice, "That's the way it works. Once you're in, you're in for life." She could feel him opening up to her, "Unless you kill them." She cut her eyes over to catch his surprised expression, and his face popped up to glare at her. Finished with the repairs, she dropped the wrench into the satchel, swinging her leg over the machine and cranking it with ease.

Standing slowly, Geek stared at her, mesmerized by the sight before him. "Who're the Dragons?" he posed the question anxiously.

Grinning at him, Tori silenced the purring engine. "*Were* the Dragons," she corrected him, "They were another group, like these guys, only better. They raised me, taught me everything they knew." She busied her hands while she spoke, kneeling down and cleaning up their mess to give a brief pause, "And when I had had enough of them, I killed them." She punctuated the comment by rising next to him to stare him in the eye.

Drawing a deep breath, his cheeks puffed out as he pointed at her, "You... you sabotaged my bike. You broke it on purpose!"

"Of course I did," she sneered at him. "You're a smart man, Geek." She lifted her chin towards him, as if in a challenge. "How else was I gonna get you away from them long enough for us to talk?"

"We're not gonna run away?" he stared at her, open mouthed in his confusion as he realized they were really going to rejoin the group.

"No. Running has no point as long as they can follow. What we need to do is find a way to clear them out. Break them. For good." She exuded confidence, and it drew him to her cause.

"All right. I'm in. So what's the plan?"

"There is no plan. Not yet, anyways. First, I need to know what you know. Why they chose you, what you brought to the table. I assume you meant Enrique, that's the guy you helped them find?" She waited for his nod before continuing. "Good. Then I need to know how you did that."

Geek looked around nervously, "Won't they be waiting for us?"

"Don't worry, we have time," she reassured, shifting to

give him a pose, "We'll catch up to them, and if things are tense, I'll smooth them over. You know I'm rather good at that; smoothing things over." She smiled coyly at him, her offer clear to any man with a real set between his legs.

Geek grinned at her, awkwardly leaning forward to kiss her. Tori relaxed at the taste of him, her hand moving up to catch him behind the neck for a moment, before visions of Max sprang into her mind. *Oh my God*, the thought made her heart leap out of control, *what if he's a virgin?* Pulling back after they shared the brief exchange of lips and tongues, she realized she would never touch him.

"You know," she laid her hand flat against his chest, "When you get home, you're gonna find some nice girl who deserves you. You hold out for that, ummk?" giving him a pat.

He looked angry, confused by her on and off behavior, so with a nod she elaborated in a gentle tone.

"You're a nice kid. You don't wanna waste what you got on a girl like me." She slid the hand up, catching the back of his neck again and tousling his hair a bit as she grinned at him. "Besides, you're more like my kid brother. That would just be gross!" Her joviality brought a smile to his face, one he hadn't worn in quite a while. "Now, how about you show me how you found Enrique, ok?"

It turned out, Geek did, in fact, know a great deal about computers and other electronic devices. Taking her inside the café, they set up his machine, and he demonstrated how he could use his laptop to locate anyone who carried a cellphone; all he needed was the number.

The thought of this scared her a little, as she thought about the tiny go-phone she still carried in her pocket, not to mention the phone Enrique had carried for over a year that she now possessed.

The implications of this technology were dumbfounding.

Explaining to him that they would have to work quietly when they got back to the group, she would want him to teach her more. She could see there was a whole other world her simple way of life had left her unaware of, and she felt eager to take it all in. She also explained that she would need his help when the time came to make their move against the group.

Nodding his understanding, Geek agreed to both conditions. He despised the Scorpions, having witnessed their atrocious acts and been powerless to stop them. "Besides, it wasn't right. It was like a trap they set for me, gettin' me to come with them and makin' it all sound so great."

Tori could see the anguish in his eyes. She could tell he carried quite a grudge, having been lured in and then prevented from leaving. *He's lucky that's all they did to him.* "No worries. When this is over, you can go home and pick up where you left off. Maybe even be a little happier than you were before." She smiled, pulling her spiral out of her bag to take a few notes as he took the time to show her more details about using the different features.

Noticing she sometimes wrote in French and German, he made an offhand comment about her linguistic abilities. "I never met anyone who spoke so many. I mean, I think Brett speaks four, and Buck three. Anyone else only does Spanish and English, like Enrique."

Tori nodded at his observation, happy he had so readily volunteered the information that might come in handy later. "The Dragons were all polyglots. That's people who speak three or more languages."

"Yeah, I know what that is," he teased her with a toothy reply.

"Meh, just wasn't sure that you did. I never knew it was so unusual until I was in the hospital after the Dragons died.

That's when I found out that speaking five languages was extremely rare, and they tested me on them. They tested me a lot actually." Her face grew grim at the memory of her time in Chicago.

"What were they testing you for?" he had grown curious about her now that he felt he could trust her.

"Who knows," she lied flatly. In hindsight, she was well aware of what the Feds wanted, and still refused to comply with their desires.

The couple remained at the diner, playing the role of teacher and student until dark, and then decided to get a room for the night. After a meal, they exited the building, and on the way by, Tori dropped her tiny go-phone in the trash can next to the door.

Arriving at the hotel room, they took turns getting a shower and dressing for bed. They had gotten a room with two, so they could each sprawl out and get a good night's sleep. Taking Geek in, as they settled into their covers, she told him about small parts of her story, trying to work herself further into his confidence.

"It was quite a shock learning who my family was," she mentioned to him absently in the dark. "The Dragons were the only one I had ever known. Except for Michael, of course." Her admission stung her, as she had been keeping his memory pushed to the back of her mind most of the time, afraid the distraction would cause her to lose her focus, and she hoped he would ignore the slip.

"Who's that?" his question seemed innocent enough, even with the name etched on her chest.

Shit. Tori lay staring at the ceiling for a moment, guilt creeping in on her. "A guy," she didn't really want to elaborate, especially since she had spent the last three or four weeks or so openly having sex with the group she rode with, and would continue to do so. "Just a guy." She hated the thought of his judging her. *Fuck me, now he thinks I'm a slut... largely because I am.* She pouted into the darkness.

Geek could tell there was more to the story, but wasn't about to pry. Instead, he remained silent, breathing deeply and thinking about home. He wasn't completely convinced the girl could help him get there, but worth a shot. He fell asleep easily, having more hope than he had felt since he had joined the group of misfits a few short months ago.

Listening to him, Tori could tell when Geek's breathing changed its pattern. Turning on her side, she stared at the door and allowed herself to think about who waited for her back in Texas. Not only Michael, Brian would be waiting for her. She knew he didn't want anything to do with her, or at least she felt confident that he didn't. Michael was her real family, and as she drifted off to sleep, she swore to herself she would keep it that way.

The next morning, the pair switched roles, allowing Tori to repeat everything she had learned back to him. She went through the steps of using the computer to follow people, performing searches on the internet, and technical parts to the device and their functions. Geek grinned in surprise at how quickly she had learned, seeming to remember everything he had told her down to the detail after only one try.

Satisfied she could run the laptop herself if the need arose, the pair packed up their things and checked out of the motel. Riding behind her new friend, Tori felt tense about rejoining the group. She knew things were going to need adjusting if she were actually going to be in a position to put her plans into action. She would need an edge and how she would get it wasn't clear.

Getting close to Vegas, the pair stopped at an old-fashioned gas station to fill up. Tori gazed around with wide eyes, *wow, this place feels familiar.* Wandering over to peer inside the roll-up door, the smell of grease tickled her nose.

She felt homesick for a moment, and continued to explore the space, a wistful expression on her features. Spying a box of junk sitting inside the entryway, she peered down into it and noticed an axe handle sticking out.

Reaching, she lifted the piece of wood, gauging it to be about a foot and a half long. She bounced it between her hands a few times, *good weight, too*. Her mind still sifting through thoughts and memories, she knew the item would make a good weapon. Calling to the kid in grime coated coveralls, "Hey, can I buy this from you?"

Turning to see what she held, he gave her a lopsided grin, "It's busted. You can 'ave it if ya want it."

"Thanks," Tori did not elaborate or argue on the bargain, and carried her new toy out to drop it into one of the saddlebags on Geek's bike.

Spying the short stick of wood, he eyed it dubiously, but said nothing, suspecting it had a purpose he would at some point ascertain. If they had time, he thought he might ask her to teach him a thing or two about fighting. And guns. *She knows a lot o' shit*, he considered her and what she had shared with him. *Not like other girls, that's for sure.*

Party Boys

By the time the two of them met up with the main group, the couple were good friends. Tori secretly wished he really were her lost little brother, and not Brian. The rally point the guys chose turned out to be a bar right off the strip, and she found herself livid when she and Geek pulled up on the side and parked his bike in the late afternoon heat.

Removing her glasses as they entered the front door, she did her best to hold a straight face. The tall man at the podium immediately asked for some ID, looking the two of them up and down. Giving him a blank stare, she opened her wallet and peeled a fifty off the stack of bills and handed it to him. Giving her a half grin, he waved the two of them inside. A quick look around, she spotted her crew, such as they were, living it up at a couple of tables along the far wall.

What the fuck? Bunch of damn party boys! Doing her best to suppress her seething anger, Tori marched up next to the group and placed her hands on her hips, left heel cocked at ninety degrees to the right.

Dan, seeing her looking fit to be tied spouted, "Wha's the matter sunshine? Think you're the only girl we can fuck?"

He had his arm around some blonde bimbo, a beer in his hand.

Giving him an icy stare, she made no reply. *I'm not jealous, dumbass*, she thought to herself, but in truth the sight of them wasting their last paycheck on the group of women made her blood boil. Giving Brett a dagger sharp stare, she spat out in German, "Job's done?"

Picking up on her displeased vibe, he only nodded, then shifted to stand. "I think it's time to move out, guys," he called to the rest. He could tell she was pissed and didn't dare offer her a drink.

Turning on her heel, she stomped past the tall man at the door, who stared after her in wide eyed wonder. The rest took a few minutes to convince, but eventually they joined her and Geek at the side of the building.

"Wha' th' fuck's goin' on here?" Buck demanded, poking Tori in the chest, "I got news for ya sweetheart, you ain' in charge here!"

Slapping his hand away from her, she stepped up, matching his height toe to toe. "Get on your bike, asshole," she growled through clenched teeth. Neither of them moved for a moment, staring each other down.

Spinning around, Tori swung on behind Brett, sliding her arms to encircle him. Revving the motor, he waited for everyone to mount up and they rode out in a line, taking the highway headed south out of town.

A few miles out lay a dirt road that veered to the left. Making the turn, the group snaked onto the back trail for a couple of miles before Brett pulled over in the pre-dark grey. They would make camp there for the night, leave any bodies behind in the morning. *Bitch pushing her luck acting like this; Buck's a big boy, won't stand for it long.* He shook his head, hoping he could avoid losing either of them in the darkness.

Parking their bikes, most of the guys started to set about making their camp, grumbling at having been pulled away from the night's entertainment. A few insinuated Tori would put out for the group like old times, as soon as Buck had finished with her.

She just leaned against Geek's ride, watching and waiting. Directly, a small fire was lit, the light licking at her face. Tori could still feel her pulse in her neck, her heart thumping from the rush of adrenaline. She kept it at a low simmer, knowing the fight was coming.

Brett had jumped off his bike first thing, headed over to try and delay the inevitable. He had always been the leader of the group on brains; everyone knew Buck was the brawn. At close to an hour of bickering, things were coming to a head.

"Jus' calm down, Buck! Ya know she's right. We got no business hangin' out like that right after pullin' a big job such as it was. Lookin' t' get busted like a bunch o' fools." He attempted to stick up for her, his accent growing thicker as he spluttered along in his excited state, but Buck refused to listen.

Tori stood tapping her foot, waiting.

"I don' give a fuck, she's got no bidness actin' like she's in charge! She even tellin' you what t' do now! But ya got yur head shove' so far up 'er cunt ya don' even see it!"

Tori glanced down at the handle poking out the edge of Geek's saddle bag, almost able to hear it calling to her.

"You take that back, ya son of a bitch. Ya know God damned good an' well who runs this outfit!" stomping his boot to punctuate his words, Brett had lost his temper, being insulted by the man who claimed to be his right hand and best friend.

Tori lay her fingers lightly onto the stick.

Buck only sneered at him, a deep laugh rolling out of his throat. "You've lost it, man. It's all over! We all work for th' whore, now!'"

As if that were the phrase she had been waiting to hear, Tori snatched up the wooden handle and sprang onto the oversized man, hitting him in the back of the neck with her weapon of choice and sending him reeling. She intended to teach him if she could, kill him if she had to.

Not going down, Buck spun around, eyes on fire as he stumbled away from her. "I'm special forces ya fuckin' bitch, ya think ya kin get th' better o' me?"

Tori exhaled slowly, in the zone and ready to do battle. "You're an old man, you fat prick. Best let it lie, before you get hurt." She laid her threat on him smoothly, pointing the end of her baton at him and knowing he wasn't about to let it go yet.

Tired of tossing insults, Buck dove at her, Tori using the small club to the best of her ability. The girl being much lighter, younger, and far more agile, he never stood a chance. A few seconds later, he lay sprawled on the sand, blood pouring from his nose and mouth while she stood over him, choking her short stick.

"Anyone else wanna show me what a fucking badass they are?" she called out loudly, the rest standing around watching the all too familiar scene. Dan shifted uncomfortably as she glared at him, recalling how close he had come to tasting the sting of her blade in Florida the first time they met.

A low murmur went up from the group, each professing their version of surrender, Brett stepping forward enough to make his case. "I guess that puts you in charge now, or do we need t' fight first?" He toyed with her, no real intention of putting up any resistance if she wanted the lead.

Tori felt an odd tightness in her chest as she realized what lay within her grasp, knowing she couldn't take it. "I don't want your place," she sneered at him, "This is your crew." She thumped her chest with her fist. "I got your back."

Turning, her hand running through her long dark mane, Tori strutted down the dirt path they had parked next to. Walking until she was a good two hundred yards away, she then stopped, looking over her shoulder to see if anyone had followed her. No one was that stupid.

Back at the Ranch

The sun sank low in the sky as Michael swung off his bike, another long day behind him. Turning to the house, it surprised him to hear the garage was silent, and he opened the door of his home to find the band lounging about his living room, waiting for his return. "Hey, guys; what's up?" He tried to sound casual, well aware something was going on.

"We're bored. That's what's up. Where the fuck do you go every day, leavin' us here alone? Some bodyguard you turned out to be," Cody voiced the sentiments of the group.

Michael nodded slowly, a quick glance around confirming that to be the consensus. "Let's go have some dinner, and we can discuss it."

The group walked the two short blocks to the diner. Making their way over to the tables in the center of the right half, they pushed two together so they would all have a seat, two chairs set to the side empty. Michael smiled at the arrangement fondly, recalling the wedding cake that had stood on such a set up only a few short months ago. Glancing at his charges, he sank into the chair at the far end, closest to the back wall and facing the door.

Trish had come right over to help with the tables, and stood ready to take their orders, chattering away about the local news. She didn't like how tired Michael appeared, *Tori's bein' away must be wearin' on him somethin' awful.*

He only gave her a small smile, seeing her look of concern, and feeling a bit guilty he kept Marge's secret from her.

The group ordered steaks and burgers and sent her on her way, turning their attention to the true leader of their group as of late. Folding his hands on the flat surface in front of him, Michael cast his eyes slowly around the small gathering. "I've been working on something," he finally relented. "Something for Tori, more or less."

"More or less," Brian cut in, "Either you are or you're not. Which is it?"

Michael glared at him, too tired to debate the issue. "I am. I'm making repairs to an old house as a surprise for her when she gets home."

"Yeah, that's what we wanted to talk about," Cody again took the role of spokesmen for the group. "We've been here four weeks. Hidin'. Nothin' to do. This town's got shit to do in it, and you won't even let us do that. We wanna go home."

Michael continued to stare, shuffling his hands for a moment. "You can't go home. Not until we receive word that you'll be safe."

"Safe?" Collin spoke up, "What makes this place so fuckin' safe? You aren't even around us, if anyone *were* to come after us."

"Well, I could always let you paint the house," Michael laughed, joking about putting the band to work on his massive project. The group fell quiet as their food arrived and everyone dug in. Looking around at the circle of overgrown boys, he felt a little guilty about the circumstances, wishing in earnest there was something he could do about it.

Taking the time to order some apple pie a la mode for dessert, the group began to talk again, the mood having lightened a bit after the meal.

Cody grinned at him, "Hey, Mike; you really gonna let us paint the house? Or at least see it?"

Michael only stared at him, taken off guard by the offer, "I was just joking about the painting," he shifted aimlessly, "I know you guys aren't really up for that." He let the four of them carry on without him, rising to head home for a shower and bed. He knew Brian would be down later, having taken up residence in the smaller bedroom, being the one they were mostly concerned about.

The other three had been allowed to get rooms over at the small motel, a huge boom in the small town boarding industry he was certain. *I guess I could let the three of them go home,* he considered as he trudged along. *After all, it's Brian that would matter, if anyone was looking.* Not ready to make the call on that yet, he wanted to give his wife a few more weeks to finish the job.

Thinking about her as he lay in bed, her tree swaying in the breeze, he wondered if she even had time to think about the men living in hiding, back at the ranch so to speak.

Just How It Is

Tori woke up before the sun, and leaned against a large rock, still a fair distance from the group. Making her way back to them, she still felt angry at what had transpired the night before. She was tired of being there, tired of being back in that rootless existence. She missed her house, she missed her friends, and she missed her husband. The time had come to get things underway.

Picking her way back down the dirt road, she found the group sprawled out here and there, sound asleep. Her gaze swinging over the group of bodies, she briefly considered the idea of whipping out her knife and taking care of them in the same fashion she had the Dragons.

She quickly realized she had dismissed the idea several times already as pure folly; they lay close enough that any struggle would awaken the others, and there would be no way to take them all out. She allowed herself a disgusted pout as she searched for the group's leader.

Finding Brett, wrapped in his sleeping bag, she dropped to her knees next to him. With a shove to the chest, she woke him with a start. Giving her a wide eyed stare, Tori shushed him with a single finger to her lips, and indicated for him to follow her. Pulling on his boots, he obeyed.

When they had enough distance between them and their still slumbering cronies, she ploughed into the conversation head first. "I've been thinking. There's some things we need to get straight around here if we're all gonna get along."

Brett only nodded, relieved she seemed so calm after the previous night's display.

"I don't wanna fight with you guys," she continued. "But I can't just stand back and let things be wrong either. You guys are way too loose for me, and I know you get what I mean. This is serious shit. We get pinched, we go to prison, or worse, and I can't take the sloppy bullshit, the party attitude. Your guys are a bunch of fuck-ups, man. Why the hell did you pick them?" Her waving hand indicated her displeasure at the sleeping men.

Brett only stared at her, feeling like he had let her down somehow. "They're just guys, Tori," he stammered, giving her a shrug. "We can't all be th' Dragons. I know you really looked up to those guys," she winced at his choice of words, "But they're gone, baby girl. This's what ya got now. And they get th' job done. So they ain't as smart, and they're a bit free spirited at times, but they'll follow orders if ya give 'em to 'em."

Tori shook her head adamantly, waving off the offer. "I told you, that's your crew," she pointed back down the road with her thumb. "I'll be your second. I can do that pretty good; but we both know no one outside this group is gonna respect me. Not your fault, not my fault. Just how it is." She looked him dead in the eye, as if she were making a pledge to him.

Brett considered her words carefully. "You're pretty amazing, ya know that?" he gave her a large grin; *I bet that guy Michael misses her perdy good.*

Making their way back to the slumber party, they began kicking the bags and stirring the pot. Poking their heads up, everyone moved to get up and get dressed, a fair amount of grumbling taking place.

Looking around at the lot, Tori realized there may be some hurt feelings at her taking second and deposing Buck after all these years. She could see him off to the side, gargling with salt water and spitting it onto a patch of cactus.

Sauntering over to have a closer look, she could see the blood as it clung to the wide pads of prickly-pair. Standing over him, she waited for him to rise, knowing it would be crucial to her taking on her new position.

When he finally stood, she could see he only had three teeth left in the front of his mouth. Squinting her eyes and wrinkling her nose in a show of mock compassion, "Ohh, that looks like it hurts."

"Yeah," he nodded, "Don' feel too good. Shoulda known Eddie trained ya up right. Guess I had it comin', thinkin' I could outsmart th' bitch who outsmarted him." He gave her a knowing glare; she may have won this time, but he had his eye on her just the same.

Tori nodded and looked away, off into the distance. She had the upper hand, and they both knew it.

With everyone packed and ready to roll a short time later, Tori swung onto the back of Brett's bike, and stroked his chest as she gripped him. She knew their time was growing short, and she hoped the opportunity to finish this job would come sooner rather than later.

They rode across to Florida from there, a long ride that gave the girl lots of time to think. She briefly considered how she essentially owned the group, as Brett would run them however she saw fit. The realization of this took her breath away, and for a short time she toyed with the idea of turning their strength against The Organization itself and eliminating them once and for all.

However, she quickly decided the act would be suicide, as the leaders were locked away in their web of protection. Besides the fact that this group, although skilled enough to pull off mundane tasks, was far below the caliber of the Dragons in many ways. If anyone would have stood a chance against that strong hold, it would have been them.

She thought about Enrique and Brett, and even Geek. They all held a great deal of loyalty towards her, the latter because he hoped she would help him escape, which she fully intended to do if she's able. He was no more meant to be with this group than herself, and if he were willing to help her, she would be willing to cut him a deal.

The former two were a bit more of a mystery. It could be because of her strength, but she suspected more than likely what lay between her legs kept them at her side. She pondered this for a couple of hundred miles, not really sure how she felt about being wanted for her assets rather than her personality, then caught a fit of giggles over her own private joke.

In the end, she longed to return to her tiny home and the man who loved her for who she was, not what she did to him in the dark. Coming to terms with that fact, she realized it would be hard for her to lay with him again. *It may take some time, but I'm going to make all of this up to him,* she promised herself genuinely. *He deserves better than this.*

Tori knew she would watch in earnest for the opportunity that would allow her to send these men on their way to join her former group mates in hell. *Surely that's where they'll be headed when I'm finished with them.*

It only took a few days, in fact, for the situation to present itself. Brett received the manila folder from the representative of The Organization in Miami, while Tori watched her first meeting taking place before her.

The middle aged man seemed a little surprised she was with the group leader, but she only gave the short dark skinned man a sly smile at his questioning stare.

Glancing through the pages, Brett asked, "How soon does it need t' be completed?"

The man smoothed his slick black strands, "The hits must all be accomplished in one night, and by the date on the corner of the file."

Nodding his understanding, Brett assured, "It'll be handled."

Deciding not to report the change within the Scorpions unless their mission failed, the well-dressed man did not want to upset things unnecessarily. Being the bearer of bad news could be a potential health hazard when it came to The Organization.

They allowed the group to leave to handle their new assignment with none the wiser. However, having a woman show up permanently inside one of the groups again would at some point need to be addressed, as the last group had ended up dead.

Mounting up the following morning, the troop headed north, out of Florida and towards Chicago. They had two full weeks to prepare, and the guys seemed confident the op would go without incident, even though Brett had announced Tori would do the planning, stating he wanted to see how she did with it.

Giving him a cynical smile, she realized he had almost made it too easy.

Arriving at a small community outside the city, the group took up residence at an out of the way campground next to a small lake, occupying a cabin and the primitive slots close to it. Once they were settled, Tori brought out a map of the city and they began to lay plans for who would take out what target, when and where.

Watching as she scribbled on her yellow legal pad and marked locations on the parchment, Brett became impressed with what he saw. *She even uses our little nerd effectively, having him scout locations on his little machine.* He gave her an affectionate grin, supremely confident he had made a good choice reeling her in, as well as the kid.

It may take her some time to really settle into our group, but she'll be happy here. After all, this's what she was raised for. And after this op, she'll see this's a good crew, too, even if we ain't the Dragons. That was, after all, the reason he had her doing the planning; so that his guys could prove themselves to her once and for all.

Taking care not to expose her distress, Tori felt deeply disturbed to see that one of the intended targets was Debra Paisley, and considered the fact that the Fed's investigation into The Organization had not gone unnoticed. She reassured herself that when her plan succeeded, Debra and the others would remain safe, as she intended to eliminate the Scorpions before they had time to harm any of the targets in the folder.

After they were removed from the equation, Tori would be free to return to Texas and to her life. She had also been thinking about her brother, and had promised herself if she survived, she would make sure he went back to his world and left her to hers. She wanted no part of his money, fame or fortune. *We've never liked one another from the time we first met in LA, and finding out we're family is no reason to change that, as I can do without him.*

As the date of the attack drew closer, Tori considered sending a warning to the Feds, but realized making contact could put the whole operation at risk. *I still don't know for sure who's really on my side within the federal entity… if one of them is a traitor, and it most certainly looks like it, I have to work this out on my own.* Using the resources at hand, she planned to do exactly that.

While making the arrangements for the Scorpions, she planned a second agenda in the back of her mind, one that would be for her alone. If all went according to plan, she would intercept the group members as they moved through the city, eliminating each of them before they could complete their intended task.

No one knew about her hidden itinerary, not even Enrique, as she did not see him as trustworthy in the end. *I hope to God this works*, she thought to herself as she laid out her secret plans on a second map, *I don't know if I can stand these guys much longer*, and it took all her resolve not to go bat shit crazy at any moment.

Marking where she intended to leave their bodies, she realized she would soon be done with them, and sighed her relief at the thought of home. Her second map complete, she hid the guide, planning to turn it over to James Godfry, and hope for the best, since Eli had basically condoned her plan. *Maybe he'll be good for something, after all.*

Set Up the Plan

The night before the scheduled day of the attack, Tori focused on finalizing the necessary arrangements, and hated being interrupted by the rest of the group. The tiny cabin they occupied had all of their materials scattered about it, the front section containing a small kitchen area with a sink, mini-fridge and microwave along the left hand wall.

The right side held a small seating area, with a couch along the front, underneath a wide picture window, facing a small flat screen television mounted on the wall. Several of the guys liked to lay around on it and stare up at the device endlessly, and she could almost see them drool as they did so.

In the center of the room stood a small table, a large map of the city lying across it with various locations marked. She had been leaned over it, working on her plans, when Enrique crept in to join her. She had run everyone out of the cabin an hour earlier, and they were all outside, sprawled about, sleeping from the indication of the snores.

She had claimed the cabin as her own, accustomed to having a bed. She wanted the one in the back room for herself, and having the quiet around her had helped her keep her sanity within the endless chaos of the group.

A couple of nights she had shared the space with Enrique or Brett, using the different ways that they thrilled her to satisfy her needs accordingly. Otherwise, she slept alone, separating herself from them the best she could while she made her plans to put them in the ground.

Not lifting her gaze when he entered, she posed a quiet question, "Is something wrong?" She had not given him any indication she was in the mood for a dirty romp, and had no intention of sharing her plans with him.

His presence unwelcome, she was prepared to run him out if he overstepped his bounds. Keeping her head down, she remained aware of his quiet movement as he made his way around the table to the hallway that led to the back, where the bathroom stood off of the narrow passage and the tiny chamber beyond.

"Jus' wanna check on you, baby girl," his tone soft, his words were guarded, "I can sees you got a lot on your mind, ya know?"

"A lot at stake here. Planning the op, making sure things go smoothly." She kept her words clean, her tone firm. *Son of a bitch, he knows this is it. I might have to fuck him, just to put his mind at ease.* She had been keeping him away from her, not wanting him to be a part of her plans, nor caring to admit he would be hard to leave behind, dead or alive.

Enrique only nodded, avoiding pushing her for what she didn't want to share. Leaning against the corner formed at the hallway to the back and the wall that held the television, he watched her as she busied herself, fiddling with the map.

Her long dark waves hanging down, hiding her scar when she peeked up at him, *God she's beautiful.* He felt his chest tighten, his thoughts filled with their future. *Our time is short, and I'll be alone again when she leaves.* He had never

149

known lonely, until she wasn't by his side. She had kept her distance from him since they had arrived in the group over six weeks ago, and he had had little opportunity to convince her of anything different.

She only chose to be close to him when she needed physical satisfaction, he no more than a play thing to her. He almost feared what her plan for him might be. *She could dispose of me as easily as she would the others.* Heaving a deep sigh, he felt almost glad, hoping she would kill him if she wasn't going to stay with him. *It would hurt less,* he rationalized.

Moving around the table, Tori gave him a pose. She knew what he was into, how he liked to fuck her. She wasn't really up for it, but she would play her part just the same. Breathing deeply, she cut him a second look, her rear facing him, her body crying out to him for attention.

The man responded to her, but she detected something different in the way that he touched her. Reaching for her, he ran his hand across her back, his fingers lacking their typical grasping manner. They were tender, soothing, his fiery brown eye's lost in thought. "You know I love you, baby girl." His voice fell deep, heavy with emotion.

Enrique had never been what Tori would have called *loving* when he held her, or when he spoke those words. Tonight, the softness of them seemed unlike him, and she contemplated how she had never seen him as capable of being those things. Nodding, "I know you do, baby." She just wasn't sure that in the end it would matter.

Allowing him to embrace her, she nuzzled his neck, kissing and breathing warm puffs of air into his ear. She guided him back to the tiny bedroom, with its small full-sized bed and single nightstand beside it, her hands moving over him calmly.

Helping him undress, she would do her part, do her best

to satisfy his desire, as it had always been. Stopping her, he gave her a small grin, wanting this time to be different. Afraid it would be his last time to have her, he wanted to make it count.

Turning off the lights in the crowded space, he left the light from the front to filter down the short hall, casting a dim glow about the room. His movements slow and deliberate, he smiled as he undressed them both and laid her onto the bed. He still faced her, his palms firm as they pressed on her skin.

Pushing at her legs, he moved to put his face against the trimmed covering of her soft folds of flesh. Astonished by his actions, Tori protected her mound with her hand, hiding her hardened point beneath it, "Don't." She gave the command softly, not intending to berate him.

"Why not?" he looked up at her with doleful eyes, confused by her refusal.

Because that belongs to Michael, she glared at him icily. He had been the only man to ever touch her in that way, to love her that much. She wanted it to remain so, the specialness of it, and of the first time he had held her, beyond words. "I don't like that," she lied flatly.

Gazing into her brilliant blue, he recalled the day he and her husband had stared each other down, across a table in a diner. *"Look her in the eye when you're with her. She deserves that."* That's the advice he had given the other man before he left him.

Too bad I never made time for it myself, too busy satisfying my own needs to worry about hers. And now that I'm ready, she won't even let me. Pushing his sadness aside and sliding up her body, he kissed her, using his lips to taste her tender neck and shoulders for several minutes before his hands moved over her, parting her legs to find his way inside.

Tori stared up at him, thoughts wandering as she struggled with his altered behavior. Lovemaking not their usual fare, his tender touch became almost more than she could bear. She rather preferred the rough and violent fucking they had always enjoyed, as she seldom had to look at him when she gave herself to him, her mask in place when she did.

I wanna get on my knees, she inwardly longed to look away, to turn her back on him. Instead, she fixed her gaze on the ceiling above him. *Like this, it's so difficult to hide,* as if he were looking too deeply within her, and able to see the darkness of her soul.

Blinking up at him, she recalled she had heard him say he loved her, *how many times? More than enough...* She had never responded in kind; never planned to. She could play the role, being his dirty girl, even enjoy it to an extent, but this was not where she belonged. She didn't need Michael, but she wanted him, and that meant more than anything Enrique could ever give her.

Closing her eyes to avoid his stare, she allowed him to satisfy himself, knowing he would fall asleep afterwards. It seemed to take much longer than usual, but eventually he finished with her and Tori could finally turn her back on him. To her surprise, he spooned up behind her, continuing to hold her and run his fingers through her hair. *Now he clings to me.*

He's afraid you're gonna kill him, along with the others. Lying still, listening to him breathe, she wondered if this had been his payment, that she might let him walk away, unsure why else he would treat her so differently in the darkness. Of course she hadn't decided what she would do yet, and probably wouldn't, until the time to make the final call.

The next morning, Tori was a bundle of nervous energy. Each member of the team had a job to do, working in pairs or as singles. Ready to lay the final essentials into place beforehand, she had announced to Brett that she would be taking Geek to set up the necessities. Having grown confident that she had accepted her position within the group completely, he didn't even question her motives as they rode away.

It only took a small amount of planning for her to be ready, and she wanted the opportunity to explain everything to her accomplice in detail, while they had time for him to ask questions if need be. Giving him the address to a downtown diner, she went over the details once more while she rode behind the thin young man she guessed might be twenty years of age, at best.

Sliding into the booth, he gave her a questioning look. "How exactly is this setting up?"

She allowed a small smile in return, then ordered a cup of coffee and a glass of water from the waitress, "We need to talk."

Her words made him nervous and he cast a guarded glance around the small space. "Were we followed?" His apprehension caused her to giggle.

"Of course not, Brett trusts me, and no one else would dare. They're all afraid of me, I think. With good reason." She noticed he gave a small shiver. "You know I'm going to take care of the heavy stuff, hun. You don't have to do anything but sit in this diner and monitor a few things for me."

Geek gave her a wide relieved grin, "Really? I was afraid I was gonna have to help. How are you gonna kill all of them all on your own?"

"Let me worry about that. But I did want to go over your part with you beforehand, just to be sure you're ready." He nodded his agreement, so she forged ahead. "We will ride out together and come here. I'll take your bike and go take care of business. You'll come inside and get your computer sct up; start tracking Enrique for me."

"Enrique? Why?" dumbfounded, he had been confident the two of them were truly lovers.

"Let's just say, I haven't decided yet what I'm going to do with him." She stirred her cup of black java nervously, and then turned her right palm to the ceiling, "I really need to keep an eye on him. I'm not sure I can trust him."

Geek nodded, not really understanding. "He was pretty upset when we found him. Insisted he had no idea where you were. Even after they tied him up and beat him." He gave a small shrug. "Not really sure why Brett suddenly decided t' cut him loose, after we spent all that time lookin' for him."

"When was this?" Tori's heart had begun to thump loudly in her ears.

"I dunno. Before we trashed that rich guy's place. Few weeks before I think. Month at the most. You guys play some serious games. I can't wait to go home."

He looked so small and meek sitting across from her, hands folded on the table; Tori knew she was doing the right thing. "Is home far away?" she asked in a quiet voice, not wanting to upset him.

"Kansas. Little town there." He didn't look up.

"You have a real name?" Truthfully curious, and not just playing the part, she picked up a southern drawl, "I'm sure yur mama didn' name ya Geek," and smiled wickedly.

"Kevin. Kevin Harris." This time he looked at her, a small curve on his lips in return.

Reaching across the table she lay her hand across his and gave it a small squeeze. "Don't worry Kevin. It's going to work out. You just watch out for Enrique for me. Ok?" She smiled broadly at him.

Flipping his hand to catch hers, he returned the squeeze. "So whatta I do? If he don't do what he's suppost to?"

"I'm going to pick up a go-phone while we're out, and

I'll give you the number. You can call me if he leaves his location, or doesn't report to it as he should." She shifted in her seat at the thought of Enrique crossing her, "I'm sure it won't be necessary, as it sounds like he's really got my back after all. Why didn't you tell me that before? That they beat him, when you helped the guys find him…"

He stared at her blankly for a moment, "I thought he would've told you. Besides, you never asked what happened. I just assumed you knew."

She studied the young man, well aware of her own policy, *never volunteer information. I can't blame him, he's right… I didn't ask, I guess I didn't really want to know.* Giving him a small grin, "It's ok. I would have worried a lot less, I think. If I had known. But, for now, we have to go. We do have a few things I need your help with. If you can, I'd appreciate it."

"Sure, I can help." He beamed widely this time, blue orbs shining.

Leaving, Tori knew they needed to be quick. First they took care of the fire escape outside Debra Paisley's apartment. Next, they headed over to the storage unit that belonged to Anthony Livingstone. After a small amount of convincing and a $500 tip, the guy behind the counter let her crack it open to take out a few things. Asking him to call her a cab, she went to rummage through the boxes and crates, confident she would find what she needed.

Making it to the front of the building as her taxi arrived, she hoisted the oversized case into the back of the minivan and climbed in beside it. Kevin would be following them over to the building, and she gave the driver the address.

Instructing him to drop her off in the alley as they reached the location, he gave her a funny look, but she only smiled. After she had her package out and leaned against the graffiti covered wall, she handed him an extra $100 and a wink before he pulled away.

Alone with her companion, Tori picked the lock to the wide metal door of the abandoned building and let them inside. She then grabbed the case of the large caliber rifle, intending to haul it up to the roof, fifteen stories in all. The bulky case wasn't much of a burden. Handing Geek the mag-light, she could carry it up the stairs easily enough, leaving him a bit put out at being given the simpler task while they climbed.

"Ya know, it should really be me carryin' that thing," he commented when they started. However, by the time they reached the roof, he huffed heavily, a bit surprised she wasn't even breathing hard. "How come you're not even tired?" he demanded as they left the weapon inside the door, so it would not be seen from another building.

"I work out," she felt a stab of pride. "Every day when I'm at home. Have done so as long as I can remember." Pushing the heavy roof access open, she made her way out onto the tar and gravel covered expanse to have a look around in the daylight.

Geek nodded. *No wonder she stomped the old man's ass*, thinking about how she had placed the axe handle into his bag before they met up with them. *She knew she was gonna confront him, and she intended to win.*

The preparations almost complete, the pair headed back down the stairs and climbed onto the bike. Stopping at a small store, Tori trotted inside to purchase the new device. She wasn't sure how long it would take anyone who might want to track her to know she had it, but it would come in handy tonight if she and Geek needed to communicate.

Back outside, she reassured him again that everything would run smoothly and the phone was just a precaution. It only took a moment for them to exchange numbers, and they were all set. Overtaken by a brief wave of affection, she grabbed him for a quick hug, and then hopped back onto the bike behind him. The sun had begun to set, and they would have a few hours to nap with the rest of the crew before the really exciting part began.

Out with the Old

That same morning, still unaware of his wife's activities in Chicago, Michael rose before the sun. First making his run, he then completed ten sets of ten, pushups, speed-skaters, and sit ups. He had begun pushing himself harder in his workouts since his love had been gone, feeling a little guilty that she had been the more adamant of the pair.

Getting his shower and slipping on his jeans, he assumed Brian would be in bed until 10:00 am at the earliest, but more than likely noon. Grinning at the thought of the band's haphazard life style, he stopped by the diner for a small breakfast and a word with his wife's best friend.

Watching the well rounded woman as she poured coffee for the locals, Michael felt a bit in awe of how hard she worked. Rarely had he been in the café when she wasn't present.

Things had not been easy for Trish since her divorce five years prior. The couple had learned a bit about the circumstances of it when Tori and Trish first became close. Left to run the diner alone, she opened the doors at 7:00 am and did not usually leave until she locked them at 8:00 pm each evening. *No wonder Marge refuses to share her condition with her daughter-in-law, unwilling to pile any more on her overstuffed plate.*

"So, you heard anything from that beautiful wife o' yurs?" she greeted him warmly, pouring him a cup of rich, dark caffeine.

"Don't really expect to," he replied as he lifted the cup and gave her a mysterious stare. Failing to get a rise from the mild mannered female, he continued with a guilty grin, "She's taking care of some business. Things from her past. She isn't really in a position to call home."

Trish didn't know much about the world Tori came from. They had never had any need to discuss the darkness she had seen in the girl's eyes the day she arrived in the quiet little town. "She ok?" she asked in a timid voice, unable to hide her concern, her tongue tied state giving her away.

"Yeah," Michael stammered, "Oh yeah. Just complicated. She'll be fine. I guess that's the thing I love about her most. Doesn't really need me to take care of her."

"She loves you though. Surely you can see that." Trish filled in for him without hesitation. Patting his arm, smiling, "Don' you worry none, hun. You know that girl'll get back t' you quick as she can."

Michael gave her a grin of agreement and ordered his meal. He knew he had a long day ahead of him and would need the nourishment. Finishing a short time later, he bid their friend a good day and headed for his current project, thinking to himself how similar the two tasks he and his mate were currently about truly were. *Out with the old and in with the new, Tori getting her life straight, and me making a place for her to live it.* The thought lifted his spirits as he faced the massive undertaking before him.

A short time later, he perched atop an extension ladder, scraping peeling paint from the side of the Victorian. Wiping the sweat from his brow, he noticed four figures walking up the short drive. He made his way down, deeply surprised to see the four members of *Indelible* standing before him, grinning excitedly.

"How the hell did you find me?" he demanded, afraid they had talked to Trish and spilled his can of worms.

"Wasn't that hard," Brian countered, "Not like there's a whole lot of places you could be around here. Besides, we took a vote and it was unanimous. We wanna help."

"Uhuh," Michael gave them a dubious stare, "You guys aren't exactly what I would call made for hard labor," he tried to be blunt.

"Hey, man; fuck you," Brian pointed a finger as he teased his new brother, "I care about her too, even if I've never been any good at showin' it." Pausing, he began to peer around, taking in the size of the structure. "Wow, this place is enormous. You're obviously not just thinking about the two of you living here."

"Maybe," Michael admitted, "But first things first. For now, it's just the two of us. When she gets home, we can discuss it further, and there might be more. It may not ever happen, but I wanna fix it up for her, just the same. Have it ready the best I can."

"So where do we start? We ain't soft ya know. We all grew up together in that little farming community in Nebraska, so we all know how to work hard when the need arises. Besides, nothing else to do around here."

The other three were quick to agree, and Michael had no choice but to put the group to work, secretly happy to have the help with the latest surprise he wanted to give the love of his life.

Run Its Course

The group rolled out a few minutes before midnight, Tori riding with Geek. He had his computer in his saddlebags, and she noted with a pleased grin that he took them straight to the diner. Watching as he set up the slim laptop and plugged it in, she tousled his hair. *Such a sweet kid.*

Images of Chris and Steven flashed through her mind, and she felt sad, ready to get home to the people she cared about and hoped were waiting for her. Forcing the thoughts aside, she knew she needed to focus.

Leaving the young man to do his thing, she pushed open the glass door to exit the diner and climbed onto his bike, riding away into the evening. Tori could feel her pulse in her throat as she rode across the pavement. *Time to let this bitch run its course.* Her palms tingled as she gripped the black rubber of the handles.

She knew this could the most important night of her life, with so many innocent lives depending on her for protection. Rounding the corner to the tall abandoned building, she picked the lock on the back door again, blocking it with a wedge of wood while she pushed the bike safely inside and allowed the door to close behind her.

Pulling out the six inch mag light, she twisted the small handle to illuminate her way through the empty structure. Reaching the large metal door that led to the staircase, she took them in twos, running the fifteen stories for the second time that day with ease, and hitting the top only slightly winded.

Making it out onto the roof, she checked her time, delighted to be right on schedule. *Thankfully I never skimped on my workouts*, she praised herself happily, recalling the climb with Geek and his obvious exhaustion.

Grabbing the long brown case she had hidden inside the door, she pulled it out into the clear area and flopped it open with a loud *fwack*. Staring down at the fifty-caliber rifle tucked inside of it, Tori knew she only had a few minutes to get into position.

Lifting the twenty-two pound weapon, she made the assembly and checked the parts quickly before sliding over along the edge of the roof. Although proficient with the device, it wasn't her weapon of choice, as she typically preferred the up close and personal touch her knife afforded her.

Waiting patiently, she knew she had about a five minute window, as she expected the pair she currently hunted to be on schedule. Time passed quickly, and the two walked around the corner of the building, stopping to stand in the street for a moment. Tori surveyed them through the scope before they proceeded down along the extended length of brick that would take them to the next corner. *Looks like they can follow orders.*

The position perfect, Tori had the first man down with a clean shot to the head. His partner, sprayed with blood, stood over his body for half a second in utter disbelief at what had occurred. His mistake, as this gave her enough time to acquire her new target and make the second shot. Not bothering to clean the weapon, she dropped it onto the case and dashed down the stairs, sliding her hands along the rail to quicken her pace.

Pushing the back door open with haste, Tori wheeled the bike out and kicked it over, eager to be on to her next stop. *Two down, nine to go, if I let Enrique live.* She still had not decided how she felt about that, and would have to make up her mind when she caught up to him.

The fact he had endured torture on her behalf swung things in his favor. *He could have just as easily rolled over on me and sent the Scorpions into Texas.* The thought of them showing up at her doorstep reminded her of Marge and her concern about hoodlums, giving her a tiny giggle, although the actual event would not have been funny.

Taking the bike up to the highest rate of speed that she dared, Tori felt free as the wind poured against her face in the darkness. She had come to love the feel of a motorcycle beneath her, the adrenaline it produced incredible. *I'm glad they actually taught me how to ride, not only be a passenger.* Taking the turns and curves expertly, she made good time.

Pulling up outside a tiny bar, Tori put on her sunglasses despite the darkness and stepped in through the back door. This would ensure her eyes were night ready when she exited the pub in short order, not having been exposed to the light inside.

Buck had been instructed to wait there, and he would be the toughest of the group to eliminate. She couldn't very well walk out into the crowd and waste him in front of God and everyone, but if she were able to catch him going to the bathroom, that would be her chance. She had twenty minutes she could wait. After that, she had to go with plan B, which would be a bit tricky at best.

He had been sitting at the bar for over an hour,

presumably drinking beer. She opened the door to the office, prepared to take on or out anyone inside, but fortunately found it empty during the busiest part of the night. She waited in the tiny cubicle, peering out into the hazy, smoke filled room.

Spying her target, his fat ass hanging over the sides of a stressed stool, *Jesus Christ, he's disgusting. There's no way he's the toughest man in this miserable outfit.* Her heart began to pound when he stood up from his perch and headed her way. Staying out of the line of sight, she watched him go into the men's room across the hall. Exiting her hiding spot, she walked in behind him.

Buck had his pants open, his rolls of gut sagging over the urinal that hung on the far wall as he relieved himself. Sensing the motion behind him, he caught a glimpse of her in the mirror to his right, and dropped his business in an attempt to swing around and face her.

His move came too late and the pop of the blade rang out a brief instant before it severed both his carotid arteries, along with his windpipe, leaving a large gurgling wound in his neck. She thought he might fight, but instead he fell over, his chin catching on the edge of the porcelain so that he slumped in a more sitting position, allowing his pulse to squirt his precious fluid out on the wall underneath it. He knew he was a dead man.

As he sat on the ground, Tori reached over to the rectangular basin and rinsed the blood that had squirted onto her hand down the drain, allowing the liquid to purify the shiny metal as well. Grabbing paper towels to dry the steel and her fingers, his eyes still watched her as she turned to leave.

Marching out of the tiny space and into the alley from the rear door, she snapped the blade shut. With a quick shove, it went back into her boot, and she swung her leg over her ride, gone before the man's heart had stopped pumping.

So far, things had gone according to plan. Three men had been eliminated, and after a short drive, she would tend to the two who would be breaking into an apartment a few blocks away. *Half an hour, plenty of time.* Tori used the rope she had hung from the fire escape to climb up, her footsteps barely audible as she ascended the metal case.

Finding the window already open a small crack, a chill tickled her spine before she slithered inside. *It's a warm evening, maybe she needed air.* Entering the living room, she surveyed the space silently, her pulse pounding in her ears like a hammer.

Not seeing anything out of place in the room, she made her way to the bedroom as quietly as she could. It stood open about six inches, so that a line of light shone across the floor. She huffed silently, aware of the need to control her breathing. *I'll be able to peek inside before being visible to anyone looking out,* but only if she were quiet about it.

Reaching the door and peering through the crack, she caught sight of a gruesome scene. On the bed lay Debra Paisley's blood spattered body. She lay naked, and the look of horror frozen on her face stopped Tori cold, her heart still thumping in her chest.

The two men had intentionally disobeyed their directive, having wanted to assault the woman before they finished her off. They had just completed the job and put her to rest, one of them still standing with his pants around his ankles as he appeared to be cleaning himself with a piece of the victim's clothing.

Heartbroken, Tori felt a flood of uncontrollable anger pouring over her mind. Pulling at her jacket, she allowed it to fall to the floor in a heap, dropping her pistol on top of it. Grasping a large cat shaped statue from the corner next to the door, she flew into the room and knocked the half-naked man to the floor. The heavy glass figure had rendered him unconscious with a single blow to the back of the head.

Spinning to face Dan, who stood gawking at her in utter dismay, she unleashed her fury. Knocking him against the wall with a few heavy swings, she tossed the effigy aside and released her knife.

Rather than cutting him and allowing him to die easily, she stabbed him in the gut, puncturing him, listening with clenched teeth to the *thock* sound as her arm shot back and forth in quick motion. She hit as many vital organs as she could through her rage red vision.

He would bleed out in short order, the blood from his liver oozing a deep burgundy, but he would have sufficient time to think about crossing her. Standing straight, she spit in his face as he stared in wide-eyed disbelief.

Tori heard the groan of the man who lay next to them. Her raw anger spent on Dan, she flicked her knife in her hand, spinning it playfully as she considered her options. *Decisions, decisions.* Kicking him in the side, he coughed as he rolled into a semi-fetal position, exposing himself as his pants were still at his calves.

Glancing over at her friend's assaulted body, she re-clenched her teeth before dropping her right knee to his chest. She faced Dan, no desire to turn her back on him, while holding her new target pinned. Twisting, grasping him firmly, she used the knife to remove his flaccid bulge with a single decisive stroke, as if it were the head of a snake.

Coming around with a horrified scream, the trapped man tried to knock her off with a shove. Clutching the bloody stump in her left hand, Tori pivoted and sank the knife into his throat to silence him with her right.

Holding her position, she allowed the blood to ooze over her fingers as she squeezed his manhood, tempted to defile him further with the trophy. Dan still watched her as his own blood soaked into the carpet, and she froze for an instant when their eyes met, her heart knocking loudly in her chest as heavy gasps escaped her.

Giving the knife a twist, she finished off the mutilated Scorpion. Her face made of stone, she dropped his organ next to him, wiping her crimson hands and blade on his shirt. Rising, Tori turned towards the bed. Catching her breath at the sight of her first female friend, the hot tears streamed down her face.

Moving closer, her chest heaved while she allowed herself a short moment to remember how Debra had made her feel like a person. Drawing a ragged breath and wiping away the drops of grief, she pulled the sheet to cover the woman that she loved and touched the top of her head in parting.

With a disgusted grimace, Tori washed her hands and knife in the bathroom basin. She could hear Dan laughing around the corner, "Guess we know what happened to the Dragons…" he taunted her, his voice raspy and faint.

Grasping the hem of her blood covered shirt, she lifted the article over her head, dropping it onto the floor before inspecting herself in the mirror. Swiftly, she removed any spatter that she could see on her skin and hair. With a snap, the knife closed and she toyed with it briefly before returning it to her boot.

Tori felt angry at herself for the random stabbing. *Jesus, did I really just cut...* she couldn't finish the thought, something so degrading, so vile, about her actions. *I guess I never realized how horrifying my most depraved self could be.* She shuddered, knowing what she would have done with the chunk of flesh if the other man had not been watching.

Returning to the bedroom, she stared at Dan through hollow eyes. She could see him taking in staggered breaths while leaning against the chest of drawers, watching her.

Reaching into the closet, she removed a plain white tee from a hanger and tugged it over her head, freeing her long dark waves from inside.

Dan sneered at her, still panting, "Ya know, your tears don' mean shit, bitch. You're goin' to hell, jus' like the rest of us, you filthy… fucking… whore."

Moving to stand in front of him, she inhaled deeply and allowed the air to pass slowly through her nose as she cleansed herself from the rush. Raising her boot, she kicked him in the face with the bottom a few times with deliberate irate thrusts. She sneered at the way the bones made a loud crack beneath the impact, reminding her of the night she had dealt with Red Farrell in a similar manner.

"Yeah, I am," she agreed with him, the blood running down his face, "But not today." Turning her back on him, she returned to the living room to gather her jacket and nine.

She exited the small apartment the way she had entered it, moving with great purpose as she descended. Climbing onto the bike once more, she knew she had to be quick and prayed no one else would be lost in her effort to put a stop to the wicked crew once and for all.

Luck was with her, and Tori found and disposed of the next two pairs and the final solo-man easily, leaving Enrique and Brett to deal with. Having seen what happened to Debra, she could hardly bear the thought of losing anyone else she had grown to love, and considered allowing them to complete their mission. If she did, she could meet them at their rally point later, allowing both men to live. That was what her heart told her to do.

You can't follow your heart, baby girl. Not this time, she admonished herself. *Too much at stake, and too much paid to stop now.* The choice tore at her in a way she had not expected.

With a quick glance at her watch, she noted that she was

still a bit ahead of schedule, and quickly considered how she might alter the plan and avoid killing the last two men. *I have a few minutes to decide, and I need to think.*

Feeling weary, she pulled up in front of the small café and cut off the engine. Taking a moment to run her fingers through her hair, she shivered, the memory of Debra's body and what she had done about it still fresh in her mind. *I am exactly what Dan said I am, and so unworthy of any other life.* A moment later, she removed her pack of planning materials from the saddlebag and made her way briskly inside the diner.

"How's he doing?" she breathed, dropping her gear on the table and sliding into the seat next to Geek. She ordered a cup of coffee to calm her nerves, waiting for him to respond as she studied the screen.

Giving her a sideways glance, he appeared surprised to see her so soon, but he supplied what he knew. "He's at the shop, been there all night," then shook his head, "I don't want you t' kill 'im."

Unable to stem the urge, Tori threw her arms around the young man, "I'm gonna try not to, honey." Feeling the relief of having made the choice flow through her, she clung to her new friend as if she were in danger of being sucked away into a murky vacuum.

"What about Brett?" he queried when she eventually released him.

"Naw, you know he has to go. We can't have him running around to come after us, now can we? He's head of the group. Odds are, he'll rebuild if we don't take him out." She stared into his blue eyes, waiting for him to take her words in.

Eventually he nodded. "So what happened?" his question seemed out of line, and he hoped it didn't piss her off.

"What do you mean?" her brow furrowed slightly, caught

off guard.

"I dunno. You seem upset, like somethin's wrong, but you're hiding it." He stared at her, waiting for her to decide if she would share the bad news he knew she concealed behind the shadows in her eyes.

Tori drew a deep breath, and shifted uncomfortably in her seat, unsure she wanted to reveal her gruesome update. *I can't tell him what I did; it was so horrible.* "One of our victims, the ones The Organization sent us to eliminate, was killed. Dan went in early, and they killed her."

Staring at her, Geek kept his tone soft, "I'm sorry. I can see it really bothers you." His voice low, she took comfort in his understanding.

Her guilty actions refreshed in her mind, Tori nodded, swallowing hard. "Yeah, but it's ok. Well, not ok, but it's done and cannot be fixed." She paused, unable to remove the bedroom from her mind at the moment, her hurt too new. Struggling to bring herself back to the present, she pushed on, "Listen, I'm gonna give you some money. It's time for you to go. Go home, make a good life for yourself."

She tried to smile as she pulled the envelope out her pocket; the one that the Tates had given her before she left LA. She had never touched any of the cash, knowing someday it would come in handy. Placing the envelope in his hand, she felt a little sad to see him go.

Geek took her offering, studying it for a moment before reaching into his pocket. He removed a small white card he had written on while he waited for the night to end.

"Here." His hand trembled slightly as he offered her the note, "This's my parents' address and phone number. In case you ever wanna meet up some time, or check in on me." He smiled at her, truly grateful for what she had done for him.

Tori's lips curved weakly as she took the slip of stiff paper. "Wow, my wallet's gettin' crowded," she confessed, and he gave her a funny look. "Never mind. Get lost." She grimaced, standing to shoo him away.

Rising from the seat, he grabbed her for one last hug, dropping a kiss on her forehead, and headed for the bus stop to make his way home.

Waving to the waitress for a fresh cup of coffee, she sank back down onto the cushion, trying to compose herself and decide her course of action. According to her plan, she had plenty of time to make it over to take out Enrique and Brett, leaving their bodies for their last target to find when he arrived at work.

From there, she would go to the federal building to inform James Godfry that the Scorpions had been dealt with and accept whatever consequences she faced for her actions. Opening the file to study the name of the last victim, she had another idea. *Perhaps I should put some of the pressure of this situation on the Feds after all.*

Allowing the anorexic girl to refill her mug with steaming brew, she stared at the computer screen before her. She could see Enrique's signal on the map, causing her to smile. *I can't believe how close I came to telling him I loved him,* she recalled their time in LA. Those words were still sacred to her, and not something to be thrown about lightly.

She still cared about him, glad she would be able to spare his life. *And of course, provided Brett is still with him, they are exactly where they should be, waiting for the shop's owner to unlock the door and make his way inside.*

Placing her tingling digits on the keyboard, she located the number for James Godfry, just as Geek had taught her. She opened her new go-phone and input the number with trembling fingers. Tori waited uneasily as it rang in her ear, licking her lips repeatedly. It was only 4:00 am, and her mouth went dry as she thought about what she would say to the man she had not spoken to in so long.

He picked up after a lengthy amount of time, obviously groggy at having been awakened from a sound sleep. "Hello?"

She heard his familiar voice, and licked her upper lip again, her own barely above a whisper. "Hi, Jim. It's me, Tori," she managed.

He sounded confused as he tried to come to terms with who was calling him and the lateness of the hour.

Thinking quickly, she tried to explain, "Listen, Jim; we don't have time for this. I need you to call someone. His name is Thomas Godfry, and I suspect he's a relative of yours." Hearing him gasp, she knew her suspicion had been correct.

"Shshshsh," she soothed into the device, "We *really* don't have time for this. You have to call him, right now. Tell him not to go in to work. You have to trust me. And I need you to come and meet me here, and I'll explain further."

She gave him the address and flipped the phone closed. Tori knew she would wait until 6:00 am where she sat. After that, she would presume he had not done as she had requested and would meet her partners in crime at the rally point as they had previously arranged, dealing with the two men as she knew she would have to when the time came.

Sitting alone while she waited, she rubbed and stretched her fingers anxiously. *Thinking about her isn't going to help,* she reminded herself. *Not now.* She still had a job to do, and would need a clear head. Pulling a list out of her pocket, she used the computer to double check the addresses one last time.

I still don't know if or when I'll ever need this stuff, but at least it'll be ready if I do. Maybe I'll give it to Enrique... The thought made her feel guilty once again, as if the act would be like paying him off.

Half an hour later, James Godfry bolted through the door.

Sliding into the booth across from her, he hissed, "Mind telling me what the hell is going on? And how the fuck do you know my brother?"

Folding the yellow page, Tori placed it back into her inner jacket pocket. She sat up straighter and appeared calm as she sipped from her third cup of joe. She seldom drank anything other than liquor or water, but tonight she needed the warm liquid to soothe her frazzled nerves and felt grateful that it had.

Reaching, she lay her hand on top of the file folder, and slid it over to the balding man, tapping on the front with a long extended finger.

Opening it, Godfry only perused a few pages before slapping it closed again and staring at her demandingly, "Well?"

Lowering the top on the computer before her with a snap, she gave him a quick rundown of the events in New York and her meeting with Eli. Jim raised an eyebrow, as if he had been left out of the loop on both events. Tori nodded, suspecting as much. She indicated the folder he possessed, "That's the file from The Organization. It contains all of our assigned targets."

Jim appeared stunned at the news. "In here? They sent you after these people?" He stabbed the folder with a stubby appendage as he spoke.

Looking down at the table, she nodded slightly, aware of what this meant, "Yeah, they did." Lifting her eyes to meet his, "You have a leak, Jim. I'm almost sure of it." *I only hope to God you aren't it.*

"Maybe," he half-heartedly agreed, then spouted angrily, "Or maybe you're smarter than I gave you credit for..." his voice trailed away as she stared at him in obvious shock. "How do I know this wasn't your doing?"

Clamping her jaw shut, Tori gritted her teeth. "You

don't. Other than, I swear to you, I had nothing to do with putting this… thing… in motion. I have been trying to stop it, and to deal with the men who were to carry out the hits."

She began by explaining how she had infiltrated the Scorpions, and further clarified that she had taken over the group, and they had all been eliminated except for the last one, who waited for his brother at his small shop.

Jim wore a horrified expression on his face, suddenly glad he had at least called his younger brother to warn him to take a sick day and hoped that he had complied.

A tear spilled from her eye as she relayed the events that had occurred involving Debra Paisley, and he considered for a moment that Tori was not the cold hearted bitch he had always taken her for. Recalling the conversation he had had just a few weeks prior with Robert Frost, he almost felt guilty at the picture he had portrayed of the young woman who sat before him. Almost.

"So are you going to finish this?" he demanded.

"As soon as we leave here, I will meet up with Brett, the last living member of the group. He will be dealt with and it'll be done," she replied without hesitation. She half expected to be arrested after this latest killing spree, but he made no mention of his intentions and she did not ask, as it was a moot point at that particular moment.

Handing him her map, the one she used to plan the op, she felt weary, as if the folded parchment were made of lead. "These are the locations. The places you will find the bodies are marked, same as before."

Godfry stared at the folded sheet for a moment before relieving her of the information. "Come to my office when you're finished," he instructed. Picking up the file and tossing the map inside, he clutched it under his arm, leaving her to her work and exiting the diner as quickly as his short fat legs could carry him.

Time Will Tell

Brett and Enrique had made their way into the tiny shop knowing it would be hours before their target arrived. It seemed funny how the pair had become real friends only in the past few weeks.

Funny considering they had ridden together for six years prior to that. *Something about the girl, maybe. Could be she's a witch, after all*, Brett chuckled at the thought. They pulled up chairs in the back to relax until it drew closer to time for the action.

"You think she did a good job, planning alls of this? I mean, we seem to be here pretty early, don' you think?" Enrique had a nervous twitch in his gut, suspecting Tori would use the op to make her move against the group, and anxious about becoming one of her victims. *She didn't ask me to help; that's a bad sign.*

"Yeah, she did a real good job, actually. An' us bein' here early's a good thing. Less likely anyone'll 'ave seen us comin' in at this hour, and it'll get busy aroun' here soon. Smart plan really. Real good job." Brett nodded, proud of his girl, and still convinced of her happiness with him and his crew over all. *It'll work out, and she'll see how good they are*, he reassured himself once more.

The younger man nodded, lost in thought about the few weeks they had spent with the group. *Maybe I should warn him. 'Course if I do, that means he'll retaliate against her an' if this ain't the time, she won't get another chance.* Sitting up straighter, he tapped his foot a bit fretfully in the dark, torn between his options.

Brett dug a smoke out of his pocket and used his zippo to light it, then popped it closed with a flick of his wrist. Taken with the need to fill the silence and keep themselves occupied, he continued the small talk, "So, ya got yur problem worked out I guess? Or ya still feelin' like she owns you?"

Enrique snorted, "Oh yeah, she owns me." Leaning forward, elbows to knees, he pressed his palms together. "Not much I can do about that. It's ok though… bound to happen sometime. An' hey, it's not like she's some delicate little flower or whiney ass bitch. Naw, she's badass, man. Tough, smart, if she was loyal that'd make her damn near perfect."

Brett stiffened slightly, "What makes ya think she ain't loyal?"

Inhaling deeply, Enrique looked over at the outline of the other man, "Wells, I ain't saying she's not exactly." *Shit…* "I'm just saying she's damn hard to read."

"Yeah, but what woman ain't?" Brett laughed, still refusing to think she would ever make a move against him. *She's loyal… enough.*

Enrique's teeth flashed briefly in the dim light, "I know, right? Time will tells, I guess." He didn't want to say any more, already feeling like he had betrayed her trust. *I still love you, baby girl, even if you can't say the same to me.*

Where Loyalty Lies

Rising from the vinyl covered bench, Tori wasted no time returning the computer to the storage compartment on Geek's ride. Starting it, she made her way over to the small shop a few streets over. Observing the row of businesses, people were already beginning to move about the area. She pulled to park around the corner and trotted down the alley to find the right entrance.

Opening the back door with her small set of tools, she called inside, not wanting to inadvertently become the victim. Her companions presented themselves from out of the shadows, where they had been hiding.

Stunned to see her at their assigned location, Brett demanded loudly, "What the hell are ya doin' here? We got this handled!"

"Yeah, well, we got a problem," she glanced around nervously, before swinging into action as she made her move against the group's senior member. She had expected him to put up a fight, but he went down easy, unwilling to raise his hand against her, even to defend himself. The pop of the blade seemed extraordinarily loud, as Tori kneeled with her knee pushed into Brett's chest.

The knife frozen above her head, she stared into his deep green eyes. The first time she had lain over him, pretending to be his lover, flashed into her mind.

Fully aware that she intended to kill him, he stared up at her with an open mouth. He breathed deeply, studying her clear blue pools. *If this's what fate's got in store for me, I can take it.*

Returning his gaze for long seconds, her still poised hand began a slight tremble, and she found she could not take the course that prudence dictated. Somewhere in the days and weeks with him, Brett had joined the men who scripted their names across her heart, and her head would lose again.

He had told her they made her cold hearted on purpose, and she knew she would have to be to complete this act of treachery. Without anger to drive her, she just did not have it in her to complete the task.

Lifting her gaze, Tori saw the pained expression on Enrique's features, uncertainty in his deep brown eyes. He wasn't going to stop her, and simply stood waiting to see what she would do.

Heart pounding, she realized she wasn't going to kill either of them. She lowered her weapon, clicking the release that snapped the blade back into its cover.

Leaning forward, sliding her legs so that she lay across him fully, she kissed the man beneath her. Nuzzling him with her nose and cheek as she exhaled against his warm skin, her silky hair cascaded around them, and she became lost for a brief moment in the closeness of him.

Rising and holding her hand out to him, she hoisted Brett to his feet and slapped him on the back reassuringly. With a silent curl of her fingers, she grinned slightly as she beckoned for them to follow her.

Outside, they walked briskly next to her as she spoke to

them in a commanding tone, "Get on your bikes and leave town. Don't ever look back," she stopped at the corner, staring directly in front of her. "Find a new life. The Scorpions are all dead, except the two of you, and The Organization is out of all of our lives for good if we leave this one behind."

Enrique tried to protest, but she brushed him off with a wave of her hand, refusing to look at him as she walked away. *Leave now*, she commanded her body to move, *while you still can.*

Reaching out, he grabbed her, spinning her to face him, "Listen to me!" Searching her features, he tightened his grip on her upper arms. "Come away with us. I can make you happy, baby girl. I know I can. You don't need that guy." He moved his hands to the sides of her jaw to cup her face, his thumb tracing the bottom of her scar as he forced her to look him in the eye.

Brett shuffled uncomfortably next to the couple. "What guy?" he inquired loudly, still in shock after his near brush with death, followed by the kiss he did not understand.

"The guy on her chest. The one in Texas," his loud voice dropped to a whisper as he spoke again to her with a small shake of his head, "You don't need him."

Hanging her hands from his forearms, Tori held onto him for a moment. Her lip trembled, and she traced the line of them up to grasp his hands, she stroked the hairs across the backs of his with her thumbs.

"Don't you know how hard this is for me? Losing you all over again? I *have* to do this, baby. I have to go home." She pulled away from him, wiping at the tears that had escaped and streaked down her cheeks. Remembering her list, she reached into her inner pocket and pulled out the piece of paper for him. "Here, take this. I don't need it," it feeling more like a bribe than ever.

"What is it?" He unfolded the yellow sheet, and Brett leaned over his shoulder to inspect it as well before he emitted a small gasp.

"Son of a bitch, are those the lockers?" Brett's eyes were wide with surprise as he studied the page of addresses.

"Yeah, that's all eleven of them that you can have. I wanna keep the one that belonged to Henry. Call me sentimental." She managed a weak smile.

"Whaddaya want us to do with 'em?" Enrique gave her a dubious look, not even sure what could be stored in them to begin with, as the Scorpions had never had any such things.

Giving him a small shrug, "I'll let you decide. Brett knows what they're for." He nodded at her with a half-smile, surprised she had merely handed them over, but they were of no use to her. She was done with that life.

Gazing at his handsome features, Tori moved as if pulled by some unseen force. She leaned forward and kissed Enrique deeply, her heart in shreds. Catching the nape of his neck with her right hand, she briefly allowed her fingers to caress the dark waves, finding it hard to say goodbye. *You should have walked when you had the chance, baby girl.*

She had kept her distance from him this time, only taking him when she couldn't resist any longer, as he was a drug to her. An addiction she had to face, and her efforts hadn't been enough. She could scarcely breathe when she whispered, "I did love you, baby. But this is how it has to be."

The man in Texas who waited for her would be less flashy, but definitely was the one she felt destined to be with. Reaching up to touch the spot on her left breast, the one now covered with Michael's name, she turned her back on them, her boots clicking as she strolled down the sidewalk, leaving the two men to peer after her in stunned silence.

Enrique moved to catch her again, but Brett reached up, grasping him by the arm, "Let 'er go, man. Ya got nothin' she needs." Pulling his arm free, Enrique gave him an angry glare before Brett finished, "Neither of us do."

Not able to agree, the younger man simply turned and shook his head, watching as she reached the bike.

Tossing her leg over the seat, she kicked the lever with an angry motion, feeling exhausted and ready to be done with the chaos. Riding downtown, she found the federal building that Eli had taken her to from his apartment over a year ago, her mind clouded by the ghosts of the past.

The glass doors weren't locked, and she made her way inside. The security guard at the counter glanced at her as she came in, and she waved. "Jim Godfry's expecting me," she called across the small foyer.

Having seen the agent enter a short time before, he gave her a small nod and motioned her straight over to the elevator.

Finding Godfry on the large black board with white letters, she punched the button to go up. As soon as the doors opened, she climbed onto the lift and leaned against the wall as they slid closed, her face in her hands and willing herself not to cry. Regaining her composure, she selected the floor and waited.

A moment later, the shiny metal parted, and she stepped out into the narrow hallway, making her way down to the correct number. Locating the spacious office, she found the man sitting in his oversized chair, nervously awaiting her arrival. Standing, he made his way over to close the heavy door, indicating for her to take a seat in one of the two guest spots that faced his desk.

Studying her for a moment, he finally asked, "So, it's really done? The Scorpions are gone?" She only nodded, not trusting her own voice at the moment. "What about The Organization?" he continued. "You need help or can you take care of them on your own as well?"

181

She had been staring at the box of tissue in front of her, and her head snapped up to look at him. Confused, she spoke in a low tone, "What do you mean by that?"

"That's your job isn't it?" He stared at her gravely, "That is the purpose you were raised for, is it not? The Dragons trained you for a special task. Surely Eddie told you what he had planned for you. How he wanted to use you to eliminate key members of The Organization and take over the whole operation." He stared at her incredulously, unsure how the smartest person he had ever met had not figured this out on her own.

Tori clenched her jaw, considering his words quietly. She had thought about this very subject many times, and had drawn the same conclusion as the man who stood before her; the purpose that Tony had alluded to all those years ago, as she sat naked on the table in the bush camp. "*Smart as they come*," he had said, "*That's why you are here.*"

Staring at him, she recalled the night she had lain with Brett and shared her memories, and the plan that he had confirmed. Eddie had taken her, and not by some random accident. He had searched for months before finding the perfect girl to implement his plan. He had watched her and her family, waiting until the time was right, when it was only her and her parents to make his move. He had placed the body of another girl in the car with them before he burned it to cover his tracks.

Furthermore, he had sent Michael to watch her brother, in case he ever needed to play that card to ensure she would do as instructed. There had only been one thing he had not counted on when he made his plans: her.

He had discovered later how head strong she could be; the stubbornness of her spirit. Even the day he had taken her and told her she would be called Tori, he had had to beat her to make her stop insisting her name was Nikki, Nichole

Peters and nothing else. And in the end, it had been Henry who convinced her to obey.

Over the years, Eddie had continued to push her, the group and himself teaching her everything they knew. They had poured themselves into her empty vessel, and relished in the wonderfully horrible creation she had become. Heartless, cold and unfeeling, capable of such brutality, smart and cunning enough to manipulate the people around her with ease.

He had done his best to make her perfect for her intended purpose, but there had been one thing he could not change about her, and that was where loyalty lies.

Inside, Tori never gave up on the good in the world. She never wanted the role she had been given, and even in the darkness with the Scorpions, when she had chosen to drink and give herself to them of her own free will, she knew she would never have walked that path if she had not been pushed down it by necessity. She would never have raised a hand against them if she had not been forced to by their own actions.

"I'm not going after The Organization," she told him in a monotone voice. "They're no threat to me, and I'm going home." She said the words as if she meant them, but deep down, she knew she could be sent to prison for what she had done that night. Somehow, she didn't think that would happen; she could make things ugly in a very public way if they pushed her.

Standing, Tori made her way over to the door. "I want my freedom," she stated as she reached for the handle. "You make that happen." Her eyes laid the threat on him coolly, and she did not need to elaborate. Leaving the luxurious office, she headed down the hall and stepped onto the elevator.

Leaving the building, she rode Geek's motorcycle to the

bus station and bought a ticket to Dallas. From there she would make her way to Abilene, and south on the highway until she arrived in a small town that lay out of the way, in the middle of nowhere, filled with people she loved.

Business at Hand

Three weeks later, Godfry stood at his desk, shuffling through the stack of papers and arranging them into the proper folders. Hearing a firm rap on the open portal, he looked up long enough to wave the dark haired man into the room, "Close the door, please."

Obediently, Eli swung the cover to the wide frame and moved to stand across the flat surface from his superior.

"Welcome back, by the way," Jim extended the pleasantry with a half-smile. "How was life in the field?"

"Interesting," Founder chuckled, "And thank you for your understanding in the situation. I realize I behaved quite foolishly and was happy to accept my punishment for it."

Godfry only grunted his reply, ready to get down to the business at hand. "So, we have here an unfinished case. Still." Eli silently nodded his agreement as he went on, "But, we are closer than we have ever been. The girl is gone, at least for the time being. And she did eliminate the Scorpions, ten men all together."

"Ten?" Eli's head popped up from the folder he had been inspecting. "There were twelve of them. She confirmed that herself, with her whole flower story," he wafted his hand in the air, indicating her illustration from a year ago. "*Each group is made of twelve men*. Did she hide their bodies, you think?"

Dropping the sheet that held their pictures on the desk, Godfry shook his head. "Unlikely. The unaccounted for are Brett Spears, leader of the pack, and your guy, Enrique Dominguez. Both former SF." He paused, allowing his counterpart to soak in the information.

Eli fingered the page. Tapping Enrique's picture, he recalled the last time the two of them had spoken. *I gave him one fucking job, and he didn't even get that right,* still angry that Michael had not been eliminated. "You think she's up to something…"

"Maybe. Either way, she said she wanted her freedom. We're working on that now. We'll send La Buff to deliver the news when we're ready." A sneer crossed his face at the thought of it.

"Oh, Warren'll love that," Eli's laugh genuine, "You know how badly he wants to put her away."

"I know," Jim's voice held disdain for the most unpopular member of their group. "He never has been much of a team player."

"What about Bennet? Is he squared away?" Eli shifted his stance, considering their accomplice.

"Yes, his pardon was approved. He did his part, played it quite nicely in fact. It was damn unfortunate that her identity was discovered. Otherwise, his plan would have worked perfectly. Of course, there is another problem we need to discuss." Jim picked up another file they hadn't touched upon yet and handed it to the other man.

"Who's this?" Eli eyed the picture of the kid inside, tall and skinny, with wire framed glasses.

"His prints were all over the bike Tori was riding the

night of the deed; and the computer she was using. I figure he was with the group as well. And no, she didn't kill him, either. I already confirmed, he's in Kansas. A real mystery there, perhaps." He grinned knowingly, as if he held an ace in the hole.

"So what's the plan?" Eli dropped the folder back onto the stack, growing bored with the proceedings and ready to take some action.

"La Buff will deliver our package in a few days. You stay on top of your end. We still need that information you've been gathering." He pointed his finger at him, "You're a damned fool, you know. Ever thinking you'll have her to yourself."

Eyes wide as his face shot up to glare at his heavy set superior. *Where the hell did that come from?* Stammering to cover himself, "Honestly, sir; I have no idea what you're talking about." His heart hammered in his ears as he waited, knowing this could be a dangerous conversation for him.

"I think you do. She's not the only genius involved in this catastrophe." His head bobbing, Jim folded his arms around his wide mid-section. "She's a collector of men, Eli. The one in Texas. These three here. You. Don't get caught up in this emotionally. She's up to something, even if she claims all she wants is out."

Godfry smiled knowingly at the younger man, shaking his head, "She's not the kind of woman who could ever settle. Not for just one man, not for a normal life. That's why our offer is perfect for her. She'll figure that out, at some point. And you will, too." *At least, I hope you do,* he added silently under his breath.

Sneak Peek at Indelible

Book 5 of A New Life Series

Running his finger down the list, Enrique leaned against a wall, waiting for Brett and trying to avoid the wind driven snow. Folding the ragged sheet, he tucked it back into his pocket, cupping his hands to blow into them for warmth. *I needs to rewrite it, I guess. It's gettin' pretty worn out.* Needed to, but more than likely wouldn't. It had been written by her hand, and that made the article special, and not for the information it contained.

"Cold enough for ya?" Brett teased as he came around the corner.

"Fuck yeah, le's get some place warm!" he grinned at his friend.

Making it to a coffee shop and finding seats inside, Brett pulled out his own copy of the list, along with the other that he'd been creating. "That's the last 'ne, so we're all set."

The pair had been taking inventory of the lockers for months. Inventory and transfer of the names so that they had clear possession with access to the contents, rent paid on all for five years. "That last stash put us over four mil. I still don' see how those guys put together that kinda cash. An' the weapons. Sons o' bitches coulda started a damned war if they was of a mind to."

Enrique only nodded, fingers wrapped around his mug and gulping the hot liquid eagerly. *I wonder how she's doing.* Pushing the thought out of the way, he struggled to return to the present and focus on the business at hand. "So, what's our next move?" He still followed Brett's lead, even if it was only the two of them left. *Guess that makes me second*, he chuckled inwardly at the irony.

"First off, I say we head some place warm," Brett grinned, tossing his red curls. "Then, we pick us up a couple o' good lookin' girls, an' we settle down for a bit. Play house, if ya get what I mean. Wait an' see, more or less. Hell, we're rich fuckers now, no need o' us doin' anything stupid that'd draw attention to us, jus' in case anyone's lookin'."

Enrique shook his head, "We can't do that. She might need us, ya know?" He didn't say her name, but Brett knew who he meant.

"Man, you gotta get over that," his green eyes flashed with concern, "You said she has your number. If she ever calls, ya know I'd be right there with ya. But she ain't called, an' there ain't no use hangin' around here waitin'." *I loved her too, damn it. But she don' belong to us.* He stared at his friend for a short pause, "It's all we can do, buddy."

The younger man only nodded. *Fuck me. An' fuck her,* angry at his pain. He ran his fingers through his freshly washed waves. "I can't do anything without thinking about her, though. Really sucks when a man can't even takes a shower without rememberin' holding a girl against the wall and pounding the fuck outta her."

"Jesus, man," Brett threw up his hands, "You think you're the only one who ever los' someone? 'sides, she ain't gone forever. If we go have some fun, maybe she'll turn up again." He grinned, "Ya know how she is. She'll get tired o' that life soon enough, an' when she does, we'll be ready."

Brett tapped his list of munitions for emphasis, causing Enrique to relinquish a small grin, fairly certain he was right. *Yeah, she does enjoy the mayhem, even if she can't admit it. And the sex, can't forget how good she is at that. Or how much she loves life on the road.*

All That Glitters

The five men worked quickly to clean up their mess, the sun threatening to go down before they were ready. It had taken them three whole days to scrape and paint the enormous structure. *Waste of time, if I get my way*, Brian Madson conceded mentally, reaching for the water hose.

He and his bandmates had been hiding in the little town for six weeks, under the protection of Michael Anderson, his newly found brother-in-law. *My God, how fast things can change.*

Previous to their estate being vandalized, and their security team murdered, the band had lived a lavish life, complete with hot women, good food, and all the sex, drugs, and rock-n-roll they could want. *All that glitters, basically*, he laughed to himself. *And now we are here, living like hermits, working our asses off for a girl I don't even like.*

Of course, he didn't really know his younger sibling either, having thought she was dead for twenty years. That, and he was well-practiced at keeping people away, especially women. *If they don't look like someone I'd wanna fuck, that's exactly what they get… shoved to the cold.*

The irony of that thought struck him from the blind side, *holy shit! It's a damn good thing, or I coulda ended up humpin' my sister! A fuckin' Greek tragedy that woulda been!*

Washing the last of the paint out of their pans, his thoughts continued to churn. *Of course, now I have to make amends for treating her like shit, especially if I want to take her home with me.*

They had been waiting for her return, and Brian had become more resolute with each passing day that he would take her with him to New Jersey when everything had been settled. *Set her up in a suite and pamper the shit out of her.* However, he had not told Michael or the others about his plan, mainly as he feared they would try to talk him out of it.

Michael would want to keep his wife and the life they shared. *Hell, he's not fixin' up this gigantic house for no reason.* The other band members wouldn't like the idea either; wouldn't want her to interfere with their lives any more than she already had.

But Brian had used his time in Texas to reflect on his past, and saw that this could be a chance for him to get back something that had been taken from him a long time ago. *Our parents are gone, but I can make her life better. And have the chance to know her.*

That was quickly becoming his priority, and in the last few weeks, he had formulated a plan. *I have a huge house in Florida, my share of the place in New Jersey, and enough money, I can buy her whatever she wants.*

He didn't want to offend Michael, but he felt fairly certain this run down shack wouldn't hold a candle to what he had to offer. *Besides, she's my sister and a musician at heart... she belongs with me.*

Indelible is Available Now!

192

About the Author

Anyone who knows me could tell you, I am a friendly kind of person, never met a stranger and take up conversations anywhere at any time. I work hard, and my mind never seems to shut down, as I wake up often in the middle of the night with ideas pouring out and demanding to be dealt with. Of course that means much of my books were written in the middle of the night.

I grew up and still live in the great state of Texas where everything is bigger, where we have warm weather and a central location. I love my state, my town, and my family, which includes my four sons, my significant other, and many friends as well.

I have thoroughly enjoyed writing this story and hope that you will love reading it just as much. And of course, there will be many more adventures to come.

You can follow Samantha Jacobey at:
Website: www.SamJacobey.com
Facebook: https://www.facebook.com/SamJacobey
Twitter: https://twitter.com/SamJacobey
Pinterest: http://www.pinterest.com/samanthajacobey/

Other works by Samantha Jacobey
http://www.amazon.com/-/e/B00GEB5LX0

Summer Spirit Novella Series - no one EVER had a summer romance like this… Charlie visits another plane, parallel to our own, where Summer Angels and Dark Angels battle over the fate of man. A unique twist on an old idea that will keep you guessing; will Charlie and Clarisse ever find their HEA? (New adult)

Irrevocable Series – from affluent beginnings, BAILEY DEWITT's life has become a broken mess... after her parents died unexpectedly, she didn't think it could get any worse. But when the arrogance of man catches up and puts the entire world into a dooms-day spiral, there will be only ONE PLACE she can run to... the ONE PLACE she wanted desperately to escape.... (New Adult)

Teach Me to Prey – in this standalone thriller, JASON TRUITT and his friends have gotten their way for years. Deceit, sex, and foul play aren't normally covered in the curriculum, but they're doing whatever it takes to get under BECKY STEWART's skin. When one of the boys turns up dead, it's a race against time to save the others; a STUNNING STORY that will get your heart racing and leave you breathless by the end… (New Adult)

The Wicked Awakened – a Halloween novel, a five hundred year old witch wants to turn SARAH MATTHEWS' body into her new home… A twisted tale involving a coven hell bent on seeing that she succeeds. Who will come out on top in this epic battle of wills? (Mature read, 18+ for sexual content and violence)

www.ingramcontent.com/pod-product-compliance
Lightning Source LLC
Chambersburg PA
CBHW030332180626
46810CB00003B/1326